ADAM EXILED

Book II

Adam X Universe

As a fan of sci-fi, I really enjoyed the imagination
in this story. An exciting adventure enveloped by
a captivating mystery. There's a lot of wonderful
references to pop culture (and beyond), which is so
thrilling as a reader. Do yourself a favour and go on a
journey through this portal as a fascinating tale awaits!
A terrific entry point into a larger universe.

Lyn – Amazon ★★★★★

Outstanding, classic sci-fi, with twists. I was caught up
in the story from the beginning! As it progresses, we
discover that not everything, or everyone, is exactly
what they first appeared to be! The result is a non-stop
roller coaster ride through time and space. I would
definitely recommend it to anyone who enjoys a good
classic sci-fi adventure story!

Ron Mac – Amazon ★★★★★

The characters were grounded and well fleshed out,
and the main character likable enough in a very
human sense. What I mean by that is he has flaws and
can be annoying at times, but that's what a human
is to me, and I can identify to the thought processes
that make him that way. I am intentionally being vague
because there are many twists and turns. My only
gripe is that I wanted more! When it ended I was
saddened as I just wanted to keep reading.

Doren – Amazon ★★★★★

I really enjoyed this book! I had never read this author before, but will be again. It has it all. Horror, suspense, fantasy, humour, sorrow and even a little love. Adam X is highly recommend.

Ravenkim25 – Apple ★★★★★

A much-needed breath of fresh air and a credit to the authors. I like the unique turn of phrase and the pace at which the book progresses. Adam X isn't your typical hero, but you'll find strong elements of Joseph Campbell's hero's journey in the arc of the text. I couldn't put this book down. Thank you, for your enthralling world and captivating story!

Robert Gennari – Amazon ★★★★★

A fantastic book that's very entertaining! The authors have a great sense of humour and an amazing imagination! I really enjoyed it.

Mikita Andrea – Apple ★★★★★

Witty, pacy, vivid and fun. I love this genre, although I usually experience such stories as this at the movies rather than as a read. I couldn't put the book down and it had me laughing out loud. I'm looking forward to more of Adam X.

Sara Vidal – Goodreads ★★★★★

Created and Illustrated by
NICHOLAS ABDILLA

Written by
**NICHOLAS ABDILLA
& CHRIS STEAD**

Edited and Designed by
CHRIS STEAD

Produced by
KATE STEAD

Published by
OLD MATE MEDIA
www.oldmatemedia.com

DEDICATED TO SOREN, MY SENSATIONAL SOUNDING BOARD

FIRST EDITION

ISBN: 978-1-925638-60-8

PROLOGUE

Once upon a time, on a remote planet in the Milky way galaxy called Flora One, there lived a young girl named Eve'E.

The lands she called home were vast and covered in enormous wildflowers that reached into the skies like green-gold spires. For those beings living in the lavish ships above the clouds, the planet below appeared to be a lush garden utopia.

For those trapped on the surface, however, far below the blanket of beautiful petals, the world was a long way from paradise.

Eve'E, like all Florans before her, was born into a life of servitude. Her days were filled with toil and struggle. Her soft, gentile frame tested daily, perfectly suited to the delicate task of mining pollen from the wildflowers.

Native to Flora One, the pollen's chemical composition had a unique and devilish power. Once mined, Eve'E's alien overlords – the Paracas – used it to concoct an illicit drug called Elixir for trade across the galaxy.

Despite the drudgery of everyday life, Eve'E did have one thing she could always count on to lift her spirits. The unconditional love of her father, Kai'N.

He was a tall man with pointed ears that poked through his long, knotted hair. Each strand as dark as night as they framed his face and fell upon his broad shoulders. He always wore a short beard, which gave him a menacing facade.

Those who knew Kai'N though, knew those muscular arms were built for one task; hugging his beloved daughter. Oh, how she loved to be held by him.

Kai'N was, in fact, a kind man and deeply spiritual. His belief in the Great Cosmic Scales gave him the strength to endure the hardships he and his daughter faced daily. He also believed it was his duty to instil this faith within his only child. So that when she looked up towards the heavens on a cloudless night, she would not just see her oppressors hovering above in their mighty ships.

She would see the stars. And maybe, just maybe, she would see hope.

On many a cold night, as they lay hungry and sore from working the stem fields all day, he would hold his young daughter close. She would rest her head on his chest and find comfort in its steady rise and fall. Then Kai'N would whisper gently in her ear a reminder: "Take heart, my child. The more we suffer today, the more joy there will be waiting for us tomorrow. For in the end all Scales must be balanced."

And as always, his voice would comfort her. The sound of his mighty lungs drawing breath and the steady rhythm of his heart would lull her to sleep.

Sometimes, his embrace would even make her forget the metal ring locked around her neck. The shock collar that was a constant reminder that her life was not really her own. She was a slave. Property that could be discarded without notice.

Kai'N spoke of the Great Scales often, and not just when life seemed at its worst. On the rare occasions something good would happen he would warn her: "Stay wary my little Eve'E. Getting your heart's desire comes at a cost. The Scales must be paid; for happiness as well as sorrow."

Eve'E thought of the Scales often in those early days. She imagined them as a person. Some kind of all-seeing, all-knowing creature who watched over them. Perhaps a dark avenger, veiled in shadows, whose sole purpose was to ensure joy and sadness were dealt out in equal measure.

In her dreams she would see this saviour holding the Paracas accountable for their crimes. This magical being would balance out all the joy Elixir had given the Paracas and turn it into the deepest and darkest misery. And she would laugh as they were punished for all they had done to her and her people.

But then she'd wake up and find herself alert and uncomfortable on Kai'N's chest. It always ended up being just a dream.

And so, over time, her hope began to erode. She found she could no longer secret herself away in the corner of her imagination and pretend everything would be alright. Her dreams began to fade as real-world experience became all-encompassing.

It happened slowly at first, but then became faster and faster still. Like rocks rolling down a hillside, pieces of Eve'E began to fall away.

It wasn't long before she began to scoff at the Great Cosmic Scales.

In adolescence, she came to realise her father saw them not as some shadowy avenger who would bring vengeance to the Florans, but as a force of nature without direction. A series of probabilities that meant nothing bad or good could last forever. His belief was that, sooner or later, one must inevitably give way to the other.

Eve'E recognised the wisdom in that and it gave her comfort and hope for a time.

When Eve'E was a woman fully grown however, she no longer put much stock in either version. There was no dark avenger; there was no Cosmic Scales perpetually seeking balance. Just her nimble fingers, stem fields and endless supplies of pollen. A realisation that only made the days darker and the skies bleaker.

Eventually, Eve'E couldn't remember the last time she had smiled. Or dreamt. Not even her father's whispered tales, or his long, strong arms wrapped around her like a warm blanket, could bring her a moment's peace.

A life enslaved had slowly banished all light from her soul. Where once hope had rested, a pit of despair now existed. She was born a slave and would die a slave; of that she was certain. Just like every other pathetic beast the Paracas had permitted to live on Flora One.

Her search for hope had given way to hate. It grew inside her like a parasite.

Eve'E loved and respected her father, but he was wrong. Dead wrong. If he truly thought some magical cosmic scales would really balance out their lives in the end, then all he deserved was her pity. And it was time he knew that.

One day, after her meagre morning rations had been lost to vermin and she had been forced to work a triple shift on an empty belly, Eve'E finally exploded.

She asked Kai'N what good could possibly come from serving their Paracas overlords. Soon everything came spilling out. Years of frustration. Of desperation, anger and oppression. Falling out of her like the water pooled in the wildflower petals above when blown by a strong breeze.

The bad they had lived through could never be balanced by any amount of good. It was beyond bad; it was evil. There would never be time to undo it all.

Eve'E couldn't stop the torrent or volcanic rage that spilled out of her in that moment and continued to berate her beloved father.

Yet Kai'N just smiled knowingly, creasing the dirt and grime baked into his face. That smile, which once calmed her as a child, only enraged her now.

"Yet if I had not been forced to serve the Paracas," he finally said, keeping his tone as even as possible. "Then I would never have met your mother. And we would never have had you, my beautiful daughter."

She remembers how that had given her fleeting pause, allowing silence to fill the void. As she remembers the voice that she heard inside.

No! You will not calm me. Not this time.

Thinking back on that moment, Eve'E would later wish she had hugged her father one last time. Or told him how much she loved him. But she was far too angry; too confused; too tired to think rationally then. Instead, she unleashed the bitterness and pain that had been building inside her.

"I wish you hadn't had me!" she screamed, ignoring the hurt in his eyes. That look, it was the only time she had seen him truly hurt. And that look would haunt her for the rest of her days. But at the time, Kai'N's reaction had only served to fuel her anger.

Eve'E yelled and cursed her father for bringing her into such a cruel world. She attacked him for daring to mention her mother, who had died not long after Eve'E was born. She even went as far as to accuse him of failing to keep her alive.

Then when she could no longer stand to look at her father, Eve'E stormed from the small alcove they had shared her entire life, leaving Kai'N with her parting words: "I hate you!"

That was the last thing she would ever say to her father. A regret she knew she would carry through to her dying day.

What she would give to see the life that could have been if she had turned on her heels and run back into those big, strong arms. Put her head against that curly-haired chest and let his loving heart soothe her pain once more.

Instead, too stubborn to return home that night, Eve'E had snuck into the pollen refinery and found herself a corner to curl up in. As she drifted off into a restless sleep she wished to her dark avenger, the Cosmic Scales and her dead mother, that everything and everyone on Flora One would go away forever.

And the next morning, they had.

XXXX

When Eve'E awoke she was disorientated and confused. Emotionally drained, her mind had wrestled with horrible nightmares all night. Visions that seemed so real still flashed through her mind even as she tried to grind the sleep from her eyes with balled fists.

For countless heartbeats, she couldn't work out where she was.

The familiar surroundings did little to help her adjust. She took in the forest of green around her and immediately recognised the stem fields. What she didn't remember was how she had gotten there? What happened to the pollen refinery? And more importantly, where were her clothes?

For one terrifying moment, Eve'E feared the worst.

Kai'N had warned her of what could happen if she was caught outside at night. Stories of ancient fire lizards snatching up the unwary! Tales of lost children lured into the dark fields by strange songs, never to be heard from again!

On her darkest days she would even wonder what it would be like to be eaten by a fire lizard. To be swallowed alive. But then she would feel guilty imagining her father's anguish and all the extra work he would pick up due to her absence.

But fire lizards were the least of her worries when she had run from her home the night prior. She knew the Paracas had wiped those beasts out long ago to ensure their slave workforce was safe. Their giant, half-buried skeletons were the only proof the creatures had ever truly existed.

She knew the true danger of Flora One wasn't found in fables, but in her fellow slaves. They could be crueller than the alien overlords they served.

With little else to occupy their free time, some of the younger men would often band together to entertain themselves. They would fight for sport and gamble away their paltry rations. On rare occasions they would even corner a helpless young woman to satisfy their carnal desires. She knew it was true; she had seen the results time and time again. The bruises. The cuts. The tears.

But the masters cared little for what slaves did to one another so long as no one was killed.

Pregnancies were always welcomed as an opportunity to increase the workforce, but dead slaves meant a drop in productivity. Anyone foolish enough to slow the production of the Paracas' precious Elixir would know about it quickly enough. An agonising jolt in the neck courtesy of their shock collar would just be the start of their suffering.

Eve'E would never forget the confusion that knotted her mind in that moment. What had happened to her? Why was she naked? Were the Paracas already torturing her father?

The last look in Kai'N's eyes as she had yelled at him flashed into her mind then and she winced as if her heart had been stabbed by a dagger. Eve'E knew then that, despite their disagreement the night before, deep down she could never really hate her father.

She shook her head, trying to throttle the vision from existence and to clear the confusion from her mind. She began working her hands up her body in search of bruising or any other signs of abuse. A few times she thought she felt something and her gut would lurch, but they all turned out to be nothing.

Eve'E let out a giant sigh of relief in that moment when she knew she had survived the night unmolested. But that sigh had turned to a gasp when her hands reached her throat.

It was gone! The collar that had remained firmly clamped around her neck for as long as she could remember had been removed.

Adrenalin surged through her body as she clutched her throat to be sure. She tried to look down, but her eyes quickly tired from the strain. Her mind raced. "This can't be!" she had thought. What was she going to do? The Paracas would zap her for sure.

It was a thought quickly followed by the obvious realisation that they couldn't zap her without the collar.

Was she free? Actually free? The urge to run had come at her like an angry pollen wasp. She could make for the mountains, or the dead lands, before anyone could find her. But what about her father? What would they do to Kai'N when they found out she was gone? Would they blame him? No doubt someone heard them yelling the night before.

Should she go back for him? But maybe the Paracas already knew? Maybe they could tell when a collar had been removed and were already looking for her?

A thousand thoughts fought for control over Eve'E's mind until one sullen realisation finally surfaced. It was so quiet. In fact, it was dead silent.

The sun was up; well up. So, where then were all the workers, getting about their daily grind? The stem fields had never been this quiet. And as that realisation began to focus her mind, it also became clear she had never been to this stem field before.

She knew every bend and twist; every fallen petal decaying in the dirt; every rock formation thrusting up from the earth. This was the only place in the world she had ever been and she knew it better than anyone. And something just felt… off.

That was when she felt truly terrified.

With practiced ease, Eve'E climbed one of the giant flower stems. She pushed past the yellow petal canopy above and up into the fresh air. It was always beautiful up there. Especially in comparison to the muggy, claustrophobic conditions below.

Eve'E gave herself a second to enjoy the breeze and the feeling of direct sunlight as it soaked longingly into her sheltered skin. She breathed it in and then slowly opened her eyes, letting them adjust to the brightness.

Eve'E shuffled to the very edge of a colossal petal and gazed out over the horizon to try and get her bearings. You could always make out the towers of the pollen refinery from up here. But this time there was nothing out there to help establish where she was.

She couldn't see the refinery or the slave barracks. Her gaze shifted higher and with it, so did her puzzlement. Not a single pyramid-shaped mothership hung in the sky above her. There was nothing but a blanket of bright yellow flowers stretching off as far as the eye could see.

She was all alone. Had the Paracas left her? Is that why the collar was missing?

Eve'E didn't think there could be anything worse than being a slave, but the thought that she could be stranded here all alone quickly proved otherwise. This was all too much.

Paralysed with fear, Eve'E almost missed the movement behind her. When she eventually turned towards the noise, she saw something pushing through the petals above the adjacent stem. Was it a worker? Was it Kai'N coming to find her and save her and forgive her? Or was it the Paracas coming to punish her and clasp a new collar around her neck?

She took a tentative step forward, which proved to be a mistake when a stem-hopper suddenly burst through the petal. She knew it instantly by reputation, even though she had never seen one in person.

Her gaze settled on its protruding lower tusk and the saliva dripping hungrily from the tip. Its fiery eyes looked straight at her and she waited for it to pounce. To end her short-lived freedom before she had even had a chance to understand it.

But instead of leaping for her it yelped in fear and bounced off in the opposite direction. Seconds later a torrent of flame shot up through the space it had just occupied. Eve'E caught a glimpse of dark scales moving below and instinctively dived for cover between the petal folds. Whatever it was, it was bigger than any living creature she had ever seen.

Eve'E remembers how violently she had trembled then, waiting for death to come.

Out through the burning wreckage of the next flower it emerged, a sight straight out of legend. A fire lizard, glorious in its splendour. It let out a giant shriek in frustration and leapt in the direction of the stem-hopper. The wind from its wings beat the surrounding petals back and Eve'E barely kept herself from falling hundreds of feet to the ground below.

Then in an instant it was gone, and she was left with no sound but the beating of her own heart in her ears.

She lay hidden for a time, rocking beneath her petal as the sun rose higher in the sky. Her head felt like a puzzle with all the important pieces missing. How did those monsters get into the stem fields? Two dangerous beasts in a matter of moments. There weren't meant to be any dangerous creatures in the stem fields, let alone one that was long thought extinct. Yet there it was, back from oblivion and threatening to send her there in its place.

She lay in that petal for hours. Thinking. Crying. Questioning. Had the entire workforce been wiped out by the beast? Is that why the Paracas had left? What had happened here while she slept?

"Why is this happening to me?" she had whispered to Flora One.

And silence answered.

XXXX

Over the next few months, Eve'E had struggled to survive. With little else to occupy her time and her father always at the forefront of her mind, she found herself once again dwelling on the nature of the Great Cosmic Scales. If they were a real thing, what had she done to make them tip so drastically against her? Were the Scales really a metaphorical construct, or was it instead a living creature like she believed when she was young?

What if the Scales were alive and had seen the way she had treated her father? Perhaps they were determined to show her how much worse life could be. If that was the case, they could consider their point proven. She would never take for granted what little she had again. Assuming she would ever be allowed to return to her former life, that is.

Then there was the other possibility; the one she dared not think about lest the floodgates open and cause more tears to fall. She had wished for Flora

One and everyone on it to disappear and her wish had been granted. Was this what the Scales thought she wanted? After a lifetime of hardship, had she sabotaged what little happiness she had with one reckless wish?

One particularly lonely night she found herself praying to the Scales for a second chance. Chased away from her paltry dinner of mushroots by a stem-hopper, Eve'E took refuge under a fallen flower hungry and desperate. She promised never to stray from the path again if only she could know peace one more time before she passed from this life to the next.

Then she began to cry uncontrollably. She knew it would give away her position to the seemingly endless supply of sharp-toothed creatures that had moved into the formerly abandoned stem fields, but she no longer cared if they found her.

Eve'E realised she was breaking at that moment. Falling to pieces. Giving up. Soon enough a fire lizard would follow her sobbing, and its teeth would pierce her flesh. Soon this nightmare would end.

But it wasn't a monster that arrived, it was Adam. From out of the darkness his hand outstretched. His small, rounded ears and his strange language. Stubborn and determined. And so very brave.

The Scales had answered her prayers.

Her time with him had more than made up for the pain and suffering of her youth. The joy he brought her confirmed once and for all that the Great Cosmic Scales were real. With her faith once again restored, however, she also had to resign herself to the inevitable truth. One day the Scales would tip against her again.

That is why, after three happy years with Adam, it came as no surprise to Eve'E when the best day of her life, quickly turned into the worst.

Chapter 1
EVE

A smile creeps slowly across my face, a reflection of the immense joy I feel inside. Shifting my weight backwards against Adam's sleeping body, I try to wiggle even closer to him and he grunts in response.

Adjusting his arm, I feel the power in his bicep as it shifts beneath my head. I twist in my limbed enclosure, the roof of our little ramshackle hut rolling past my vision until my head rests on the perfect spot. Right there, in the centre of his chest.

Oh, to be held by a man once again.

Lying with Adam I feel content and happy in a way I never imagined possible. My head relaxed in the fine hairs that dust his torso, I float to the rhythmic rise and fall of his breath and listen to the slow steady beating of his heart. I can't help but notice how peaceful he looks when sleeping. The X tattooed on his forehead smooth and free from the worry lines that too often crinkle his brow when awake.

Looking at the mark on his head reminds me I too have been branded with a symbol. What did Adam call that shape?

A figure eight.

Or the number eight perhaps? But why would I have a number eight in the exact same spot he has a cross. I've always felt Adam might know the answer to that riddle; he certainly seems to get restless whenever I bring it up. When the Preservers captured us and held us captive on their ship, why did those horrible beasts feel a need to brand us so?

I find myself rubbing at it as if doing so will somehow make it disappear, then curse myself for letting such a small annoyance distract me in this perfect moment.

I must enjoy this happiness now before the Scales tip back.

Of course, the mark will never leave me, but I do manage to wipe a few beads of sweat off my brow. I notice a faint sheen of perspiration still clings to Adam's flesh as well. Exhausted, he had no trouble drifting off into sleep, but I was unable to join him. I remained too excited. Too energised. It was amazing. Being connected to him in such a way. I know I've only just made love for the first time, but I already want to do it again.

You finally have your man, Eve! It took three long years, but he's finally yours.

Pressed against him under the warm fur blanket, I think back to the bizarre set of circumstances that brought us to this place.

When I first laid eyes on him, we were in an artificial habitat on board an alien spacecraft. Not that I was aware of that fact at the time. The illusion was so convincing that when I woke up naked in the stem fields, I thought I was still on Flora One. The planet that had served as my home and my prison.

It never even occurred to me that I'd been abducted by the Preservers.

By the time Adam and his android companion Anne had found me, I was caked in mud and practically feral. Confused, lost and cheated out of dinner by a far stronger and better equipped predator, I'd basically given up.

The last thing I ever expected was for Adam to appear from the shadows. The last thing I expected was help of any kind.

Even half out of my mind, I remember thinking how handsome he was. That sandy shoulder length hair and those deep blue eyes. Even when I realised he wasn't Floran, it did little to dissuade my initial impressions of him.

Didn't Anne say we were practically the same species anyway?

She told Adam that the Floran race began when the Paracas started enslaving Humans and relocating them to their Elixir refineries on Flora One. From what I have seen, Humans and Florans are practically identical apart from one minor inconsequential quirk.

One that is easy to overlook at first glance. Floran ears have evolved a slight point at their top.

Not that you can see the tell-tale points under my thick red locks.

Whether that small change occurred as a result of natural evolution from generations spent on a planet other than Earth or was a side effect of genetic tampering by the Paracas, I will probably never know.

I'm not really sure I want to know.

Thankfully, this one small difference never seemed to bother Adam. And it definitely didn't change how I felt about him. All I cared about was that he was brave and kind, and warm to the touch.

Even those silly little ears of his are cute.

When I was a stranger to him, he literally gave me the clothes off his back and a place to rest. When we were attacked by a fire lizard and I twisted my ankle he risked his own life to carry me to safety. And when we finally came face to face with our captors – and The Hunger, a truly awful, shockingly dangerous parasite – he shielded me from danger and made sure I got into a drop pod safely.

By the time we had escaped the Preserver ship and made it to his home planet, Earth, I was head over heels in love with him, even if I couldn't articulate those feelings at the time.

I wonder why I couldn't bring myself to thank him then and there?

I hadn't spoken to anybody for months by that point and I think I just couldn't bring myself to start. The last time I had spoken I had not only struck sorrow into the heart of my father, Kai'N, but tipped the Great Cosmic Scales against me in spectacular fashion. Perhaps I thought keeping quiet would prevent me from making the same mistake.

Then there was Anne. She was so strong and knew so much. She was better than me in every conceivable way. Perhaps I thought if I opened my mouth, Adam would realise that truth for himself.

Looking back now, it almost feels as if it were all a dream. Him saving me when I was broken and helping to put the pieces back together.

He reminds me of a hero from the fairy stories father would tell me as a child.

Being with him as we first set foot on the shores of Earth was almost enough to convince me happily ever afters really do exist. That the Great Cosmic Scales could shift forever in my favour.

But unfortunately, shortly after our arrival, our perfect ending took a tragic turn for the worse.

Adam quickly discovered the home he had fought so desperately to get back to was nowhere to be found. The Preservers had abducted Adam during his world's twenty-first century, but when Anne piloted the ship back into his home dimension, she did so six thousand years too early.

If that wasn't bad enough, Adam then learned The Hunger – the highly intelligent parasite we had faced while making our escape from the Preservers' ship – had also managed to free itself from captivity. Even worse, it was on its way to devour everything on Earth.

It seemed like all was lost in that moment.

I will never be able to wipe The Hunger from my memory, no matter how hard I try. The way it both drowned and dissolved a Preserver right in front of our eyes was the stuff of nightmares. Thinking about it now sends an involuntary shiver down my spine.

Seeing our captors die like that almost made me feel sorry for them, even after everything they'd put us through.

With nothing available to combat the threat, Adam's android companion had no choice. Anne turned herself into a bomb. She made the ultimate sacrifice to save us, and an entire planet, from certain doom.

Adam took the loss hard. Those first few weeks he was inconsolable, and, for a time, I thought I might yet again have to fend for myself. I had no idea what to say or how I could help him. And the truth was, I didn't really understand his distress.

Not that I was silly enough to say that to him.

No matter how lifelike Anne may have appeared on the outside, underneath that unblemished skin and perfect hair she was just a machine.

An annoyingly beautiful machine to be sure, but still just nuts and bolts.

Admittedly, it was unfair to suggest nuts and bolts held Anne together. She was head and shoulders above any of the previous artificial life forms I'd encountered. The Paracas overlords who had enslaved my family used robots for personal security back on Flora One. I remember one Paracas bragging that his clunky metal bodyguard was worth more than a hundred slaves. So, I can only imagine what they would pay for something as sophisticated and lifelike as Anne.

Those bastards would probably trade an entire mothership for a piece of tech as cutting edge as Anne.

But Anne was gone, and I knew Adam's grief had nothing to do with monetary value. It was more likely he had become attached to her in the time they spent together and had started to think of her as a real person. Possibly even a friend.

At least I hoped that was as far as his feelings for her went.

Whenever I tried to broach the subject, he would conveniently decide it was time to start conserving power on his Universal Translation Glove. Which would only make me more curious.

Back then, the UTG was our only means of communicating with one another and it hadn't escaped my notice that he turned it off every time I started asking uncomfortable questions. Eventually I took the hint and just stopped asking about Anne.

But even though Adam was being evasive where Anne was concerned, his insistence that we stop relying on the translation technology ultimately worked in our favour. Not using the UTG all the time forced us to learn each other's languages, and after a few years we barely needed the device at all.

I do miss those lessons, though.

There is a certain intimacy to teaching one another a new language. I enjoyed the back and forth as we took turns naming objects and then repeating them to one another. It brought up feelings of exploration and discovery. Great feelings. It was then that I first began to acknowledge a bond was forming between us. A closeness unmatched by anything I'd ever felt before.

Well, until tonight at least.

I learned English faster than he did Floran. I was putting together full sentences while he was still struggling with the basics. I was probably more motivated to learn than he was. Seeing the way his face would light up whenever I spoke new words in his native tongue was all the incentive I needed.

Picturing that smile in my mind's eye pulls me from my reminiscing. I slowly reach out and run a finger over his lips, feeling the little imperfections burnt into them by the desert sun. I briefly consider leaning over to kiss him and perhaps encourage more love making, but think better of it.

No. Better to let him sleep. He doesn't sleep enough as it is.

No sooner has that thought crossed my mind when I'm overcome by an uncontrollable urge to cough. I try to choke it back, annoyed at the horrible timing, but quickly realise it's not possible. Despite my best efforts to muffle it, the throaty sound is terribly loud in the near silence of our small hut.

Gross!

Hand still clasped firmly over my mouth, I look towards Adam praying the noise did not wake him. I freeze as he murmurs something unintelligible before rolling to face the straw wall, still sound asleep.

Phew!

My stomach knots as I pull my hand slowly from my mouth to examine the contents within. I know what to expect before my eyes focus. Even in the near darkness I can make out the vivid drops of red splattered across the pale skin of my palm. The rawness in my throat had already given it away. More blood. The happiness Eve felt only moments ago peels away like a scab, exposing the ruined Eve'E that lingers underneath. Fear arrives unwelcomed.

Why does this have to happen now when I finally have everything I want!?

As I brush the blood into the dirt in a bid to hide the evidence from Adam, I hear my father's voice inside my head answering my unspoken question:

"In the end, the Scales must be balanced."

Chapter 2
ADAM X

It's the same damn dream every time, like a bad television rerun playing over and over inside my head. It starts with the two of us standing side by side on the shore of a picturesque beach. Bathed in pale moonlight, I admire the beautiful curves of her face as her eyes scan the heavens. The stars reflected in her pupils; the breeze tugging at her dark chestnut hair.

Anne?

I think her name, but she doesn't respond.

"Anne!" I shout in earnest.

Then again, louder and with more urgency. But she can't see or hear me. She never can. As always, I'm forced to watch events unfold without any way of altering their outcome.

Resigned to that sad fact, I follow her gaze upwards until I see the moon and then, a heartbeat later, a secondary object. It's a quarter of the size, but equally as bright and positioned in such a way it looks like it's floating just above the lunar surface.

The Preservers' ship!

Then I spot what has captured her attention so fully. There, amongst the twinkling stars, something burns brightly as it plunges to the planet's surface. A sudden jolt of panic runs through me as I recognise what is falling towards us. A threat like no other.

It's The Hunger! If it reaches the surface, we're all dead!

As I turn my focus back towards Anne, I'm horrified to find her removing a circular chunk of skin from her forehead. She then digs two slender fingers into the newly formed hole and, after a quick twist followed by a hiss of pressurised air being released, she slides out a glowing cylinder from deep within her skull.

Her face is perfectly passive; the numbers already crunched. As I watch her snap the cylinder in half and remove a small silver ball of plutonium from within, it becomes painfully clear what she intends to do.

She's making a nuke! She's going to blow herself up!

Every part of my being screams at me to stop her. To reach out and prevent her from following through with this suicidal mission. But there's nothing I can do. In this nightmare I have no physical form. No voice to plead with. No arms with which to restrain her. All I am is a disembodied presence. A mute spectator being forced to bear witness as this selfless machine sacrifices herself to save an entire world.

No, she's more than just a machine!

Calling Anne a machine, or an android, or an artificial life form, diminishes how truly amazing she really is. Anne is as much a person as anyone I've ever known. Even more, in fact, given how I've come to feel about her during our brief, but eventful, adventures. And now she is about to die before my very eyes. Again.

There must be another way!

As the fireball in the sky continues to draw closer, something in Anne's demeanour changes. Nuclear payload in hand, her normally passive features seem suddenly concerned. She takes a moment to stare wistfully out at the waves. Her impossibly blue eyes unfocused as if lost in thought.

Anne?! Please don't do this! I love you! Stay with me!

It's always at this moment as I finally confess my feelings to her that she turns to face me. I realise then that she is truly seeing me for the very first time. Gazing deeply into my eyes, she smiles and says: "So this is love."

And that's where it always ends.

The dreams come once, maybe twice a month. They are not as common as they were at the start, but no matter how big the gap, I know they will always come back sooner or later. Ready to leave me hollowed out and miserable. This time, however, as my eyes burst open and I'm thrust back into reality, I find Eve sleeping soundly by my side.

I gasp a few breaths, letting the familiar tensions drain from my body. Then, as I watch her content face lying on my chest, a new emotion swells up inside like an unwanted tsunami. Guilt.

Adam, you idiot. What did you do?

I've tried so hard these past three years to protect and nurture Eve without crossing that line. At first, I was worried about her emotional state, as she had clearly been to hell and back on Flora One. When she first began speaking, her words were scattered and disconnected, almost broken. For a while I didn't know if she'd ever recover.

But she did.

Then I held back because she seemed so much younger than me. A silly thought for a clone to hold onto, really.

Technically, I've only really been alive for just over three years.

Once I realised the age gap wasn't as big a deal as I first thought and I could no longer use it as an excuse,

I started telling myself what was really holding me back was fear of ruining our friendship.

God, that sounds like the biggest cliché ever.

Eve is the only other person on this planet I can talk to and the fear of losing that was terrifying. The other humans in this era are so primitive by comparison and who knows what would happen if I actually tried to mingle with any of them. I've seen enough science-fiction movies to know that changing the past can cause terrible things to happen to the future.

So, Eve and I, we had to stick together. I was afraid that if I let things get romantic and it didn't work out between us, I could wind up truly alone for the first time since I woke up in my enclosure on the EDN.

I also got the impression that I'd be her first and wasn't sure I deserved that honour. Especially given that it was still Anne that haunts my dreams.

I guess it's too late to worry about that now. What's done is done.

Staring up at the weaved reeds that comprise our ceiling, I slowly exhale and try to untie the knot of anxiety building up in my stomach. Eventually my racing mind begins to slow down and after a minute or so I'm feeling a little better.

I turn back to Eve and attempt to look at her without letting fear cloud my judgement.

She really is beautiful...

That pixie face of hers and that waifish, yet attractive, physique. Those cute freckles and that strawberry blonde hair. As I marvel at the way it cascades over her soft shoulders, a stray beam of sunlight cuts through a gap in the reeds. It strikes her beautiful curly locks and turns them such a deep red they look like they could burst into flames at any moment.

...and she's funny, too!

If I was being honest, her sense of humour and sarcastic wit are often the breath of fresh air I need in this otherwise gloomy existence. When she finally began talking, she grew back into the woman she must have been before she was kidnapped and cloned eight times.

Not that I've told her about the cloning yet.

I imagine she must have been strong before being isolated from her father and alone finally wore her down. I almost had a mental breakdown myself and I had Anne. I was never truly alone. So, for her to survive by herself in a world with giant fire-breathing lizards... well... it's pretty awesome!

She has my respect, that's for damn sure.

I definitely care deeply for this girl. I'm certain of that! And I know she's completely smitten with me, that's been obvious for a long time now. I'm pretty clueless when it comes to women, but even I couldn't fail to notice her less-than-subtle attempts to woo me over the years.

Surely I should be nominated for a sainthood just for holding out as long as I did, right!?

But last night she got her wish. I just hope she doesn't come to regret it. I run a finger up her arm and over her shoulder. Absentmindedly, I tuck a few loose strands of red hair behind the tip of her pointy ear.

Eve smiles in her sleep as if the touch reminds her of something happy and she shifts slightly in the warm morning air.

C'mon Adam, admit it. You enjoyed yourself last night.

I shift uncomfortably at the thought and more so when I feel myself becoming aroused. Trying to move my mind in another direction, I'm surprised when my thoughts fall on Missus Jenkins, my religious education teacher.

Ew! Well I'm no longer aroused.

Like most children growing up in my area during the twenty-first century, we were taught about the bible and Christianity. I always had my doubts about the whole thing. The tales in that old book just seemed so ridiculous, but recent experiences have had me rethinking those previous reservations. Especially that story from the book of Genesis; the one about Adam and Eve.

What if we are that fabled couple?

It wasn't the first time the question had found its way into the front of my mind, but it couldn't possibly be true, could it? Regardless of how emphatically I dismiss the notion, I can't stop the thought coming back every now and again.

On the one hand, when we landed here, Anne's original scans revealed there were six million humans spread out across Earth. Which meant that Eve and I were definitely not the first two people in existence.

But that doesn't necessarily prove it's not us, does it? Just that the writer got some of the details wrong. After all, six thousand years of Chinese whispers were bound to get a few things muddled up.

Nah, it can't be us.

If it were true though, that would mean we are actually destined to be together. And that we are arguably the most famous couple who ever lived. Imagine that!

Eve and I, the Bible's own Brangelina?

I look over at her and watch her chest rising slowly up and down. I notice the slight blush on her cheeks. A part of me will always love Anne, but she's gone now, and I know that deep down she would want me to move on with my life.

You know it's true.

Allowing some recurring dream to hold me back would be stupid. Especially as it's probably just the result of post-traumatic stress, or something like that. She didn't love me; she couldn't. And anyway, the dream version of Anne is nothing like the real thing and more like some romanticised fantasy illusion.

I mean, what's the deal with her smiling at the end? Anne never smiled a day in her life!

The more I think about it, the more certain I am that everything with Eve is going to work out for the best. I can do this. But let's not put the cart before the horse. Start small… I need a drink.

I sit up slowly, careful not to disturb our makeshift mattress of reeds and feathers. Reaching up to rub the sleep from my eyes, I'm startled when something soft brushes my cheek.

What the?!

I slap at my face in panic hoping to squish the pest then pull my hand away to see if I got it. I'm relieved to learn the intruder in question is the newly acquired bracelet on my wrist and not an unwelcome creepy crawly scuttling across my face.

I'm glad Eve wasn't awake to see that.

Eve gave the bracelet to me last night and I'd completely forgotten I was still wearing it. I take a moment to look at it more closely. The band is made of several pieces of interwoven string ranging from gold to dark red in colour, wrapped around a sturdy strip of Floran fire lizard leather. It was decorated with tiny seashells Eve had picked up during our travels along the Egyptian coast.

It's so precise and delicate that I can't help but marvel at her ability to create something this intricate with so little to work with. This was the straw that broke the camel's back; that knocked down that last wall holding me back from her. I caved in, giving her what she wanted. I gave in to what I wanted.

I should really get her something in return to show her I care, but what?

Flowers have always been my go-to gift, except I haven't seen anything pretty enough to put in a bouquet in years. The only thing growing plentifully around here are weeds and spindly little papyrus flowers. Maybe I could find a big, blue lotus?

No you knucklehead! She was enslaved on a planet full of giant flowers.

My other go-to option, chocolates, are also out of the question. If I remember Miss McGill's home economics class correctly, they're still a good three thousand years away from being invented.

And she told Mum I never listened in class!

Well she was half right. Maybe if I had paid more attention to her, I would know how to make the delicious substance. I could go out and get the ingredients and become the guy who invented the stuff. Willy Wonka sans the Oompa Loompas. But I don't remember; so, I guess I can't.

I'm just gonna have to make something like she did for me.

Sliding gently out of bed so as not to wake her, I pick my jeans up off the floor and slip them on. Since my only pair of underpants disintegrated over a year ago, I take great care when pulling up my zipper.

Learned that lesson the hard way.

I flinch at the thought. Before I tiptoe out the door, I snatch up my shirt and pistol from the bed I usually occupy, making the decision to leave behind my jacket and Universal Translation Glove.

Standing just outside the hut, I squint as the full force of the morning sun hits me smack-bang in the face and chest. It's going to be a scorcher of a day. To be fair, it's nearly always a scorcher around here.

Why couldn't we have landed somewhere a bit more temperate? Like the Bahamas?

Hopping about as the hot sand starts burning my feet, I scoop up my tattered sneakers from beside the entryway. Then I tip them over to make sure there isn't anything nasty hiding inside.

Another lesson learned the hard way.

I quickly slide them on and tie the laces, before casting my gaze over my surroundings. I probably should have taken a good look around before putting on my shoes. What if a wild animal was out here? Or one of the primitives that roam these lands?

Can't afford to get complacent. This is a dangerous time period we're living in.

But like always, the little village remains deserted. My eyes fall over the seven huts, built in a roughly circular fashion, and I wonder yet again why the previous inhabitants abandoned such a perfect location. This encampment's close proximity to not one, but two separate rivers makes it the ideal place for a group of humans to thrive.

Who builds all this then just leaves it behind?

When Eve and I first moved in we would spend hours speculating over what happened to the original inhabitants. Foul play was ruled out almost immediately as there were no signs of violence or any dead bodies left to rot.

Well, there was one dead body.

A dead goat to be precise, whose skeletal remains were still propped over a cooking pit.

"Well, I'm pretty sure that one was murdered," I joked at the time.

And was probably delicious, too.

One day, when exploring to the south, I came across a cave with some cryptic drawings on the walls. It showed what appeared to be the village and people fleeing from a bright light at its centre, fear etched in their faces. Two moons sat in the sky and serpent shadows curled out of the clouds. It made little sense.

In the end there just wasn't enough evidence to discern why the original villagers had vanished. Over time the subject came up less and less, and my diligence regarding village security with it, apparently.

Truth was, after two years of wandering aimlessly through ancient Egypt and the Middle East, we were both just grateful to find somewhere to call home. Hopefully nobody ever comes along to dispute our claim on this place. Not that I envy anyone stupid enough to try bullying us into leaving.

> *That reminds me, I should check how much charge I have left.*

Examining my gun, I can't help but marvel at the plasma pistol's design. The sleek, futuristic weapon is made entirely from a tough silver metal that I'm not entirely sure exists on Earth's periodic table. It's super light and scratch resistant, and hasn't displayed a single dent despite all the accidental knocks I've given it over the years.

In fact, it looks as new as the day Anne stole it from the Preserver ship. I've tried to use it sparingly, turning to it only as a last resort when catching food. Thankfully, I've never had to fire it at a fellow human.

Ejecting the green stun clip, I am satisfied to find it's still two-thirds full. Clicking it back into place, I tuck the pistol into my waistband, then tie my shirt around my head like a bandanna. It covers the X tattoo on my forehead, not that anyone I come across in this world would understand its meaning.

"Hi, I'm the tenth clone in the Adam Furst line. Nice to meet you."

I wonder if the Preservers ever made an eleventh Adam?

It would seem unlikely. It had been years since I heard the recording sent by my Kréken friend, Zanatos, from the Preserver ship. The message warned us of The Hunger's escape and descent towards Earth, and I'll never forget his parting words.

"You have made an impression, friend Adam," he said. "The new Eldest seems intent on writing the past wrongs its race has committed."

I hoped that meant the Preservers would stop stealing people from their homes and cloning them for their alien zoo.

I wonder if they built another Anne?

"No!" I berate myself. We did this already today. I'm done with it. I'm moving on. I grit my teeth and with some effort push all thoughts of aliens, androids and cloning from my mind.

I managed to convince them what they were doing was wrong and that's the end of it!

Shrugging it off, I walk to the centre of the village. A broken rib sits jammed into the ground like a tent peg next to our still smouldering fire pit. Bending down I pull the sun-bleached shard of bone from the dirt and turn it over in my hand.

The arrow bone, as we've come to call it, originally belonged to the very same goat we found when we first arrived here. The remains had long been picked clean by scavengers and the carcass was a bit of an eyesore. I had just started clearing out the remains when I found the broken piece of rib laying near the pit. Now it serves as a primitive GPS tracker.

Goat Positioning System.

I devised this idea whereby we could use the bone to inform each other where we'd gone whenever one of us wandered off on our own. With that in mind, I lay the bone down with the pointed end facing in the direction I planned to travel. There, now she won't worry about me when she wakes up.

Well, not worry as much, anyway.

West, by my best reckoning anyway, to the closest watering hole.

A shriek from nearby grabs my attention and I look towards the shrill sound. It's a vulture up on a sand dune; never a good sign.

The day prior we'd caught a plump boar in one of the spike traps I'd set down by the river. Catching the animal was an amazing stroke of good luck and the resulting feast was the best feed we'd had in ages. Practically a celebration.

There's no doubt a full belly contributed to last night's outcome.

I had actually forgotten about the boar till just now. What happened after we ate it? There was eating; there was touching; there was kissing. And then we went into the hut.

So, where did the carcass go?

My eyes fall to the ground and I see the marks for the first time. A scattering of paw prints and signs of something being dragged away. I follow the marks but know full well they travel in more-or-less a straight line from the cooking pit to the large bird of prey.

Cautious now, I move in its direction. The vulture looks up from whatever it's feasting on and stares at me, still and ominous. As I close the distance between us the scavenger hops away moving to a respectable distance and watching me with baleful eyes.

It's the wild boar carcass alright, rotting in the morning sun. Judging by the paw prints and the way the poor creature has been gnawed, it must have been dragged here by a leopard while Eve and I were otherwise occupied. I shrug at the sight. The thick stench brings tears to my eyes, but I can't help but acknowledge how death no longer fazes me.

Funny, something like this would've really grossed me out back in the day.

The remains make me think about Anne again and I find myself recalling the day she caught a similar beast. I can still picture it perfectly. Her deceptively strong frame lugging a boar through the waterfall concealing the entrance to our cave. And my efforts to choke back vomit as she began to carve it up right before my eyes.

I learnt so much about living off the land from watching her.

Suddenly I remember the scars we found on that boar's stomach. M, I and X. How did I forget about that until now? I didn't realise it at the time, but that must have been the creature's cloning number. Just like the one the Preservers used to mark me.

If I'm remembering my roman numerals right, that would make it... one thousand and nine.

I can't help but chuckle at the thought and wonder what unintentionally smart aleck remark Anne would have made had she learnt it took me three years to unravel the mystery.

Running the imaginary interaction in my mind, I feel myself starting to sadden again. But caressing the bracelet on my wrist and thinking of Eve prevents me from sinking too low. I glance back at our hut and reaffirm my commitment to her. It's finally time I stopped living in the past.

The night you died I made you a promise, Anne. That I would honour your sacrifice by surviving. But I don't think that's going to be enough anymore.

Long ago, in some other life, Adam and Anne may have had something amazing together. But in this time, in the here and now, Adam Ten and Eve Eight have a real chance at building a future. Creating something new; something special.

I think it's finally time for me and Eve to stop just surviving and to start really living.

Turning away from the boar, I look back at the vulture and its impatient gaze. "It's all yours, buddy!"

I scoop up one of the numerous ceramic jugs left behind by the previous villagers and head out towards the river.

May as well get some water while I'm off checking the nets.

Chapter 3
SOBEK

A small motion of my hand is all it takes for the men on my left to begin moving forward. I watch on near breathless, tension knuckling my shoulders so hard I can already feel the beginnings of a crick in my neck. As their bodies scythe through the undergrowth, every unnatural movement in the tall strands of grass accelerates my heart. But in truth, I shouldn't be so worried; my men are well practiced.

They move like the breeze.

I cast my eyes forward again to ensure our target remains naïve to their presence. The man sits by his fire, talking that gibberish language from the bowls of Duat as if communing with Osiris himself. The woman repeats the words back to him, struggling to wrap her mouth around their complexity. It's the same ritual every night.

You'd think with those long pointy ears she'd be able to better hear what he is saying.

I should be counting my blessings that tonight the man sits with his back to the south. There's more cover from this direction and we need to be on him before he knows we are there. Who knows what powers Set has granted these white demons? His unusually pale skin looks as black as a shadow from this angle, the fire's flames licking around his shape.

I cannot fail.

It had taken several months to convince the elders that we must take the fight to these two intruders. Some in the village had argued the man was attempting to communicate with us and that we should listen. But as warriors, we knew we could not allow a being of such power to reside this close to our homes. Stories of the pair's arrival had flooded in from the east, with each storyteller's eyes wider and more scared then the next.

One woman swore there had been a third demon who had arrived with the others and disappeared just as quickly. This one had the body of a woman but the hair of a man. I'd retold the tale to my men as we prepared our attack lest they need any further incentive to strike and to strike hard.

"I saw them come," the woman whispered upon her arrival in our village, eyes vacant. "They fell from the sky. Three of them! Skin pale like the moon and speaking with a demonic tongue. I will never forget their hair. The man's flowed like sand and the woman's burned like fire. Then the third one, who was neither man nor woman, struck the man of sand and took off so fast it was a blur. Faster than the fastest horse. Faster than the cheetah. Nothing from this world could run that fast."

It had sounded like nonsense and when I said as much the lady's arm snapped up to my throat and pulled me in close.

"Look at my face," she wheezed. "Look at it!"

Up close I could finally see beneath her hood. The left side of her face scared beyond comprehension, as if it had been melted. Her ear was all but gone and her hair singed in such a way you knew it would never grow back.

"What weapon from this Earth can do such a thing to a person?" she continued, and I had no answer to fill the space as she paused. "Because moments after that devil ran off, a fireball erupted in the sky with such a sound it bent the grass flat against the sand and pulled trees out of the ground, roots and all. But that wasn't the worst of it."

She relaxed her grip on my throat then, but I had stayed in close where I could be sure I wouldn't miss a single detail of what came next. Word of the fire in the sky had spread far and wide, but this was the first we'd heard of the beings that had done it.

I asked whether it was the fire that had hurt her face, but she shook her head.

"No, it was a few days later," she revealed. "I was creeping up on a young Ibex from downwind, low in the grass and ready to pounce. It's head suddenly snapped up, but it wasn't me it was looking at. No. It was that man of sand..."

It was then the intensity in her eyes turned to trauma. Her voice rose an octave and took a maniacal edge as she tried to spit out the word. Tears welled in her good eye and spit began to form in the corners of her mouth, seemingly trapping the word she was trying to say before it could get out.

"Fire!" she finally howled, and the floodgates opened. "He shot green fire from his hand. Bright like lightning it sizzled and crackled through air. Oh, Ra, give me strength. One came and startled the Ibex and as the second came it leapt for safety. The fire hit the grass on my left side and scorched the earth and my face in an instant. Oh, my beautiful face."

She began sobbing then, pulling up the skins that covered her body to show her arm was just as disfigured. Her body, too.

"A third fire came from his hand and hit the Ibex as it escaped," she continues. "It died instantly, yanked unnaturally to the side at such velocity it skidded along the ground and into the base of a tree. It all happened so suddenly, and so violently, it shocked me into silence. Not the man of sand, though. He was so happy as he ran to the Ibex rejoicing. I can just be thankfully he never saw me as I'm sure he would have finished off what he had started."

That was last week however; I need to focus on the now.

I shake the memory from my head and turn to the men on my right. Another subtle motion of my arm signals my request and they push forward, too. I can see the looks in their eyes. They're scared, but they're brave men. Their task is the hardest. By floating down the river, they'll be able to come in from the east in the cover of the reeds. The demons won't expect an attack from that side and we'll catch them in the crossfire.

If he gets a chance to raise his hand, he'll burn us all.

Just then, there is a loud crack to the left. I snap my head around, my heart in my mouth. I see Mery, my youngest son's face aghast as his eyes dart down to the small stick that's just broken beneath his foot. My eyes snap up to our target in desperate hope, but it's wasted. The man is on his feet, peering into the darkness. The woman, too. I see something in his hand glint in the moonlight.

Could that shiny stick be what he uses to make fire?

I freeze and will my men to do the same. A wind rustles through the grasses as a deathly silence falls on the land; our heartbeats thundering in our chests the only giveaway to our presence. The devil's eyes scan the perimeter.

Are we discovered?

If I act now, maybe I can save some of the men from being burned alive. I'll charge him and draw his fire while they make a run for it. The demon takes a step forward, awkwardly tentative.

He's coming.

I dig my toe into the sand and raise myself on my fingers, muscled clenched. A small movement catches my eye and I look to my oldest friend, Khufu, half-submerged in the river as he begins to flank the encampment. He shakes his head, no. But this is my fate. I must. I tense my muscles, dig my toes into the sand, take a deep breath and…

Laughter?

The demon turns back to the fire and retakes his seat chuckling. I let the adrenalin flow through my veins as I relax each muscle one-by-one. It's all I can do to prevent the men seeing the shaking now twinging down my muscles.

We stay still for a full five minutes before I give the men a nod and we continue moving forward. I throw a last glance at Mery, but if he was expecting to see anger in my eyes it wasn't forthcoming. I wish him a silent good luck and slide down the mud into the river to join the men heading down towards the thick reeds of its western bank.

Shortly, we're all in position. As the rear guard crouched in the shallows, I cast my eyes across the shoulders of the men crouched in front of me, seeking any sign of weakness or doubt. But they are strong men. And they are ready to defend our people and rid our home of this threat.

It's all on me now

Two quick Ibis honks is the signal. At the end of the second honk, we attack in ten counts if there is no change in our target's behaviour.

Now or never.

I cup my hands to my mouth and make the sounds: two quick honks. Eyes fixed on the target, I'm pleased when the ghastly conversation at the campfire beyond the reeds neither slows nor stops.

Ten. Nine. Eight.

Good everyone's ready. I flex my fingers around my spear, my eyes unable to blink as I scan my men once more. They all look ready. Legs coiled and charged, ready to swing into action. We will be swift; we will be deadly; we will be heroes.

Seven. Six. Five.

Suddenly, there is a movement in the water next to me. Like the ground itself has fallen away and a large volume of liquid has been sucked into the space.

Four. Three…

Then I'm upside down, pain rippling along my midriff and blood erupting out my throat. I look down to my stomach only to see rippled scales running along an enormous head clamped against my gut. Yellow eyes stare at me for a split second as I dangle above the water. I let out an anguished cry of pain and it echoes across the silence of the river. Immediately chaos erupts on the bank as I hear a dozen voices shouting in panic.

Then I'm slammed into the mud hard. I hear my neck snap as I'm dumped on my head and an instant numbness consumes my body. Then moments later I'm twisted through the air and my legs crunch down just as hard, snapping into shards with the impact. A spear swings past my eyes. I recognise it as Khufu's as he tries with all his might to penetrate the crocodile's tough scales.

No, don't help me. Attack the demon.

Khufu's spear is no match for the crocodile's hide, but it lets go mid-roll all the same. I fling out of its jaws landing out in the deep water. Paralysed and mauled, I suck in my last breaths as the river starts to pull me downstream. Just before it all goes dark, the world lights up. Green fire sizzles through the air.

We missed our chance.

I watch as my men scurry through the reeds running for safety, the fire shooting out across their heads. Just as they go out of sight, I see Mery alive and safe, scanning the water even as he makes his escape. And with that one blessing granted, I go still and calm as I see the stars fade away one by one.

The scales ripple the surface ever so slightly as my victor comes to finish me off. As my last breath gasps into the humid air, I'm yanked viciously beneath the surface and from this world, once and for all.

Chapter 4
ADAM X

Well that's annoying. I check my nets as soon as I arrive at the river only to discover they're empty. Staring into the crystalline waters, I curse the fish for refusing to be caught.

C'mon, where are you?

It doesn't take too long to spot what I'm looking for. A ripple, followed by the slightest splash. There are fish in there today, so they're bound to swim into my net sooner or later.

I'll just have to wait a bit longer.

This is the smaller of the two rivers that border our village. They ferry a thriving aquatic ecosystem from deeper in the desert towards the sea and I love watching the current endlessly flow towards the Persian Gulf.

Something about its relentless forward movement is calming. The way the condensation and frost collect into hundreds and thousands of harmless little streams, which funnel down to join one another until it's a mighty river. An unstoppable force.

And it's so pure; bereft of pesticides or oil or chip packets. That being said, I rarely risk going in.

I still haven't learnt to swim after all.

Thankfully there is a deep pocket of water that has spooled out to the side forming a natural well and this is where I place my nets. I remain satisfied with collecting the one or two fish a day that escape the torrents to rest in the pool's stillness. It has proved to be our best source of food since we moved in.

As an added bonus, avoiding the main river has also ensured we haven't become dinner for one of the large crocodiles roaming these waters.

What an awful way to go.

The thought conjures up memories from our brief time in Egypt. Eve and were trying to establish a home by the Nile and integrate ourselves to the locals with limited success.

One night the men from a nearby tribe came to scare us off. I never saw them coming, then all of a sudden one of the poor buggers was being savaged by a scaled beast. I fired off a few shots to shoo away the others, but all I could do was watch as their poor leader was dragged into the water and devoured before our very eyes. I still wonder every now and again if I could have done more.

No, there was nothing I could do to help him.

The memory makes me shudder and that moment was the straw that broke the camel's back when it came to our time in Egypt.

That poor guy.

With that image front of mind, I check for the tell-tale sign of scales threading their way through the water while I reset the nets.

Moving away from the shore, I plonk myself down in the shade of a palm tree and take a second to listen to the sounds of the river's rush to the south. Watching a flock of birds fly overhead, I contemplate how frustratingly monotonous life here in the Neolithic period can get. Basically, Eve and I spend most of our days hunting and gathering food. At night we eat whatever we've scavenged, and while Eve assures me she's never eaten this well in her life, I feel like it's never quite enough to fill my belly.

Back in the day if I was hungry, I could just order a pizza and someone would bring it straight to my door.

I know deep down that's not technically true. I never actually lived in the twenty-first century and all my memories from that time belong to Adam Furst, the man from whom I was cloned and whose memories were implanted into my mind. But the problem is those experiences feel as real to me as anything that has happened since my actual birth three years ago. And knowing I've never actually eaten a pizza doesn't stop me from craving its cheesy goodness.

A cold beer would be amazing, too!

With pizza and beer firmly on my mind, a mental checklist starts to form of all the modern conveniences I miss. Or at least what my fake memories cause me to miss. Coffee. Television. Air conditioning. The internet. Music. Showers. Deodorant.

What else? It only takes a second of thought and the big leaves above to remind me of an essential item that can never be forgotten. Toilet paper! I add it to my mental list and begin searching my memories for anything else. A few more come to mind before I realise this train of thought is just making me more and more depressed.

What am I doing? Not even an hour ago I was chastising myself for living in the past. Now here I am wishing I was living in the future!

Done giving myself a mental spanking, I begin once again to focus on the present and the one good thing I have in the here and now.

Eve.

Thinking of her gentle smile, my attention quickly returns to thoughts of her amazing gift. There must be something I can make to show her my gratitude. Last night was actually quite special. I think about it again and feel a rare smile tug at the corner of my lips.

And her gift deserves something equally special in return.

It's around midday when I check the nets again. The rock pinning the trap to the mainland was shifting ever so slightly, a tell-tale sign that something in the deep has made a fatal turn.

As I pull the nets in, hand over hand, I can't help but admire the strength in their construction. It's something only possible thanks to Eve's ingenuity. Somehow, she fashioned an armful of reeds into a tool capable of catching an endless supply of food.

What would I do without her?

I dare not say the thought aloud, but if there is one positive to come from Eve's former life mining delicate pollen from Flora One's wildflowers, it's the incredible strength and control she has with those cute little hands. I glance again at the bracelet, rocking slightly back and forth on my wrist with each pull of the net, with admiration.

Wow! It's truly amazing.

When the net finally surfaces, I find my patience has been rewarded. A massive carp emerges from the waterhole and with it the promise of holding back starvation for another day.

Grasping the squirming prize in my hands reminds me yet again of the fiercely loyal Zanatos. My old friend and a fellow prisoner of the Preservers. But while I still miss the big blue warrior, I don't miss the smell of his fishy armour.

I wonder what that ugly amphibian is doing right now?

Hopefully he's back on his home world, Krés. Hunting dangerous beasties and feasting with his egg mates.

The flash of a feathery shadow tells me it's time to stop daydreaming and move on. A white-tailed eagle circles above, its sharp eyes no doubt focused on the prey gulping helplessly for air in my hands. With practised ease I whip the fish against a rock once, then twice, and feel it go limp in my hands.

I reset the nets and fill the jug with fresh water from our little river. Carefully, I balance the filled container on my shoulder, then bend down to pick up the slippery carp by its tail before beginning the slow trek back to camp.

The day is hotter now and the weight of the water makes the walk back feel doubly long. I attempt to distract myself by pondering what I can make for Eve? Alas, coming up with creative ideas as never been my strong suit.

It's not until I pass the rotting pig carcass for the second time that inspiration finally strikes.

A pretty weird time to have an epiphany, but hey, I'll take what I can get.

Excitement quickens my pace and I'm soon back at the village proper. I look towards our arrow bone and notice it remains exactly where I left it. Eve must still be around here somewhere.

"Eve?!" I call out.

"In here!" she calls back, her words drifting out from the shade of our hut. As I take the fish and jug inside, I'm surprised to find her still in bed.

Strange. She's normally the first one up.

"Hey, sleepy head. You okay?" I ask her.

"I'm fine. Just tired," she replies, flatly.

She does sound exhausted.

"Fair enough," I tell her. "Well you rest up. I got us some food and there's fresh water here when you need it. I've just got one last thing I need to take care of before I start cooking. Back soon!"

"Do you need any help with it? I can get up?" she replies half-heartedly.

"No. You relax," I reply. "I won't be long."

When she nods her head dismissively and rolls over, it gives me pause. But after a brief moment, I decide I'm probably just reading too much into it and head back into the heat. After all, I have no reason to doubt her. She probably is genuinely tired like she said.

Last night was a little tiring for me, too.

Still, as I grab the first items I need to make her present – some twine Eve fashioned from stripped palm leaves and a sharp stone knife we found in one of the neighbouring huts – I can't shake the feeling that something is wrong.

Is she tired or angry?

I run everything that happened the previous night through my mind, searching for any anomaly that could stand as evidence for the latter. That she is upset with me.

Was I no good?

It's possible; the last time I had sex was… well, actually never. I have plenty of Adam Furst memories on the subject, but I guess until last night I was technically a virgin.

Maybe I was awful!

But I don't think Eve would get upset over something like that. It's not like she had any grounds for comparison, after all. I'm sure it's just my imagination running away with me.

Feeling slightly less self-conscious I decide a bite to eat will help settle my stomach. I grab a pomegranate to munch on from the tree just outside of camp. I then begin retracing my steps back towards the final item I'll need to complete Eve's gift.

The present I envision is relatively simple in design, but the reality of putting it together ends up being far more complicated than I had anticipated.

After shooing away the vulture once more, I try to get a good grip on the boar's tusk so I can wriggle it free from its jaw. It's no easy task thanks to its awkward positioning and the relentless buzzing of flies.

What I wouldn't give for a pair of pliers right about now.

The beast smells awful and tying my shirt around my face does little to keep the horrible stench of decay from forcing its way up my nostrils. Before long the sweat covering my hands makes grasping the tusk even more challenging. I begin to worry about slipping and cutting myself on its germ-infested teeth, then retch at the thought.

That's all I need.

Needless to say, I'm overjoyed when the tooth finally pops free. Confident the worst is behind me, I set to work on the next part of the job.

Using the point of my stone knife to push a small hole through the bone proves to be way harder than I'd imagined, too. Frustrated, I end up putting too much pressure on the tusk, cracking it in two and making it completely unusable.

After swearing and kicking a few dirt clods, I notice I've also managed to cut my finger in the process.

Great! Just great!

I briefly consider sticking the bleeding finger in my mouth, then, imagining all the bacteria on my hand, decide against it. Besides, the wound is already starting to close up thanks to the nanites Anne injected me with back on the Preserver ship.

For a moment, I contemplate whether cursing my luck is even fair or whether I should put things in perspective. Such a wound, even this small, could mean death to someone from this era. It's still weird to think there's millions of microscopic robots swimming around in my blood. A superpowered immune system fending off ancient diseases.

My composure back in check, I tip the wild pig over and begin the arduous task of pulling out the last tusk.

Only one more chance to get this right!

Once freed, I use the knife again, this time with far more care. Gently I dig a cavity into the long tooth, periodically flipping it over and working on the other side until the two holes break through to the centre. Some sort of organic juice, liquefied by the sun, pours out, bringing a rancid smell with it. I retch again.

With the newly formed holes complete though, I'm able to thread the twine through the tusk and to stand back and marvel at my creation. A necklace. One that can remind her of the night we ate like kings and shared our bed for the first time. I turn it over a few times, letting the sun get a good look at its shape. This is seriously badass. I hope she likes it.

Well, once I've cleaned it up a bit of course!

I take it down to the river to scrub off the gore, then decide it couldn't hurt to give myself a good scrubbing as well. I bathe quickly in the tepid waterhole, eyes ever watchful for scaly threats, but I'm spared the panic. Then I stand on the shore for a blissful moment, letting the sun's rays and hot breeze dry me off. Once dressed, I head back to camp at a brisk pace, excited by the prospect of showing Eve her new present.

Probably best I keep the details of how I made it to myself, though.

XXXX

The delicious scent of frying fish greets me well before I enter the village. It makes me nervous at first.

If I can smell it, so can the local wildlife.

Eve wouldn't know a leopard is patrolling the area and I briefly consider putting a stop to her efforts, but soon my mouth is salivating in anticipation. I hurry into the village and my eyes fall on Eve who is busy cooking the freshly gutted carp. I tuck the necklace into my pocket, deciding to wait for the perfect moment to present it to her.

"You didn't have to do that," I tell her, resetting the arrow bone then taking a seat beside her at the cooking pit.

Should I be kissing her hello now?

"I couldn't lay in bed all day," she replies, turning back towards the fire and sparing me the awkward decision. "Besides, you caught it. The least I could do is cook it. Did you notice the boar is gone?"

I nod my head, but decide not to mention the leopard just now. Why spoil our first moment of domestic bliss with the truth?

"Probably just vultures," I say confidently, scanning her face for a reaction.

And there it is. The look in her eye tells me enough to know she's seen the leopard tracks already. But to my relief she is gracious enough to let me think I'm saving her from worry.

She's not an idiot, Adam.

She is hiding something, though. Now that I'm close, I can't help but notice she's looking pale. Really pale. Her naturally light skin seems even lighter in contrast to the dark green top and sarong she wears. I knew there was something else going on when she decided to sleep-in.

Stay calm.

 "Are you alright? You're looking a little peaky," I ask, placing my hand on her forehead before she has time to wave away my concerns. "You're a bit warm, too."

She laughs, meekly.

"I've been slaving away over a hot stove, silly" she teases, throwing one of my own tired jokes back at me with a meek smile. "And if I look... what was that word you said? Pee-key?"

"Peaky; It means pale or unwell," I explain.

"Well if I look peaky, it's because I didn't get much sleep last night," she finishes, flashing me another smile, much cheekier this time.

"Oh that," I grin back sheepishly, then fumble for something to say. "Umm, last night was... yeah that... well I guess that's kinda my fault, huh?"

"You do snore terribly," she returns pointedly.

Snore? That's what kept her awake?

"I do not!" I object, doubly hurt now. "Do I?"

"No, you don't. I'm just teasing. I just had trouble getting to sleep after... everything," she says, wistfully.

"About that... was it okay?" I venture nervously. "I didn't do anything wrong, did I?"

Abruptly, she turns from her cooking to stare me straight in the eyes. Then with an expression so stern it borders on scary, she replies in a tone that could only be described as matter-of-fact. "Last night was the best night of my life and no matter what happens in the future, I don't want you to forget that."

Her words and the intensity with which they're delivered leave me completely speechless.

How do I reply to that?

Thankfully, before any sort of panic can stream to mind, Eve's cheeky grin returns and she continues to talk, saving me from having to think of a response. Although somewhere deep in the recess of my mind, an uneasiness remains.

"You worry too much, you know that?" she tells me, her voice playful once more.

You don't know the half of it!

"Besides, if anyone is going to ask someone if they're okay, it should be me," she adds. "What made you finally let your guard down after all this time?"

I dunno. A full belly and good company? Nah, you can do better than that.

"You mean other than being a sucker for jewellery?" I banter, admiring my new bracelet in an overly flamboyant fashion.

"If I'd known you could be bought so easily, I would have done it a long time ago," she teases, punching my arm. "But seriously. What's changed?"

How do I explain this without saying something I shouldn't?

I pause to give it some real thought and Eve gives me the time to think in silence.

When I finally reply, it's the truth. "I guess even though we escaped the Preservers all those years ago, it always felt like I'd left a piece of myself back on that horrible ship."

Yeah, a piece called Adam Furst.

"I realised that as long as I kept clinging on to that part of me, I could never really move on or allow myself to be happy. Last night I finally reached a point where I was ready to let that go and stop torturing myself."

There's a pause as I realise Eve is waiting for me to say more, but sadly, lamely, pathetically, nothing emerges from my lips.

"That's good, Adam," she eventually answers. "I truly believe that if anyone deserves to be happy, it's you."

Her words are kind, but I can't help but notice a tinge of sadness.

Damn it! Was she waiting for me to declare that I loved her?

But I'm not sure I'm there yet and I don't want to say it until I truly mean it. I need to redirect this line of questioning post haste.

"Hey, we both deserve a little happiness. And that's why I went out and got you a little present today." The sudden wave of tension lifts immediately.

Well played mate!

"You didn't have to do that!" she says, clearly excited despite her words to the contrary.

"I know. But I wanted to do something to let you know how special you are to me," I explain, as I fish around in my pocket. "It's important to me that you know… well… we wouldn't have survived here, I wouldn't have survived here, without you."

This will cheer her up, I just know it.

"Ta-da!" I announce, as I hold up the necklace. "It goes around your neck."

When my ears detect no squeals of glee or gasps of wonder, I shift my eyes from the gently spinning tusk to Eve's face. Her perfect little pixie face. She couldn't look more horrified.

Why does she look like I just slapped her with a wet carp?

For a moment there is no sound except for that of the sizzling fish. Eve makes no attempt to take the necklace that dangles between us, she just stares at it eyes wide like a deer caught in the headlights. She goes to say something then instead rushes her hand to her mouth. Without a word she leaps up from her seat and runs to our hut coughing and sobbing.

What the hell just happened!?

Sitting dumbfounded for all of ten seconds, I finally climb to my feet and make my way slowly towards the hut. Poking my head through the entrance, I spot her hiding beneath the covers and I can tell she's crying. Our blanket, made of camel skin, shudders in union with her body.

Remaining in the doorway for fear that my very presence may upset her further, I attempt to make some kind of sense out of her bizarre reaction.

"Eve? Can I come in?" I ask gently through the cracks in the wood. "I'm not sure what I did, but I'd really like to talk about it if that's okay with you."

"I'm so sorry," her muffled sobs reply from beneath the blanket, her voice sounding hoarse like her throat is just a bag of razor blades. "You did something so sweet and I just ruined it. I'm such an idiot."

She thought it was sweet? Well that's something at least.

"You're not an idiot," I attempt to console her. "I'm sure you have a good reason for being upset. I just really wish I knew what that was."

"It's dumb," she manages.

"Why don't you let me be the judge of that?" I prompt her. "Talk to me."

Eve stops as if considering the proposal, but with her face buried away it's hard to tell what she is thinking. Eventually, she decides to talk.

"You remember me telling you that I used to be a slave back on Flora One, right?"

Eve hadn't said much about that time in her life and I didn't want to probe. What little I do know though sounds pretty horrible.

"Of course," I reply, a sudden feeling of unease rising in my gut.

Where is this going?

"Well, I never told you this before, but the Paracas used to make us wear these collars. They used them to keep track of us and they could give us a lightning-like jolt if we disobeyed an order or broke a rule. When I saw the necklace, I just… I just freaked out. The thought of putting something around my neck again…"

And I thought flowers were the worst choice!

A clash of emotions erupts within me. The anger surrounding my stupidity is difficult to contain, but I remain calm by reminding myself this is not about me.

Still, I feel like a complete heel.

And not just because I picked the absolute worst gift ever. I also never told Eve that we are both clones, and that all her memories before waking up in the Flora One habitat belong to someone else. I wanted to keep her safe from that knowledge.

When I found out I was a clone it almost destroyed me right there and then. Perhaps the only saving grace was I didn't have time to think about it. Not like here, where we've had all the time in the world. An unwanted memory suddenly flashes to my mind.

Adam Furst in a tube.

But I shove it violently to the side. "I'm so sorry, Eve," I croak, my words heartfelt. "I had no idea. Look, you don't have to wear it. I'll throw it away right now."

"No! Please don't do that!" she pleads, looking up just enough so I can briefly see an eye above the camel skin before she turns back into her bedding. "You made it for me and I want it. I'm just not ready to put it on right now. Can you leave it beside the bed for me?"

"Okay," I tell her, placing it on the log that serves as the bedside table between our two cots. "Now why don't you come out from under those covers and we can have a meal together?"

Eve moves beneath the furs and for a moment it seems like she might emerge.

"Actually, I'm not feeling very hungry," she mutters in rejection. "Do you think maybe you could give me some time alone?"

"Umm... sure," I reply hoping it sounds like I'm cool with it, even if I'm not. "If that's what you really want."

"It is," she insists without pause, keeping her face buried the whole time.

Great. She doesn't even want to look at me.

I do my best to hide the disappointment in my voice. "Okay. Well I'll be out here if you decide you want to talk some more."

I slink from the hut feeling utterly dejected, and to add insult to injury, I'm greeted by the smoky stench of burnt fish.

I guess I'm going to bed hungry as well as depressed tonight.

I plonk myself down by the firepit and briefly consider checking the nets for another fish.

I think I've lost my appetite, too.

Instead I sigh and start assembling the puzzle pieces of what just happened in my mind. There's obviously so much more about her time on Flora One that she hasn't told me. I try to picture our first meeting again. Were there any other clues there to her previous life?

*How could there be? All that stuff happened
to someone else.*

I was so sure I'd made the right decision keeping the truth from Eve. Finding out you're a clone drowns your soul in a thick, black metaphysical smog and leaves you helplessly hollow inside. You don't feel real. Like you shouldn't exist. I didn't want her to have to go through that if there was no upside to that knowledge.

But now that I see how painful some of those false memories are, I wonder if it would've been kinder to tell her she was a clone from the beginning. Then she could've had a fresh start.

But she was so shaken and frightened at first. And now… I gulp as I realise how much I've failed her. Witnessing the pain my silence has caused her I can't help but wonder if it can be reversed.

Is it too late to tell her the truth?

Not right this minute, of course; that would just be cruel. Maybe I should tell her sometime soon. But how will Eve react knowing I kept this secret to myself all this time? Will she understand why?

*I lied to her, and now I'm scared she'll never
be able to forgive me for it.*

Chapter 5
EVE

I lied to Adam and no matter how I try to justify it, I can't escape that one undeniable fact. I don't think I will ever be able to forgive myself. Sure, the necklace was a bit of a shock and it did bring up bad memories from my days as a slave. But that's not what brought on the tears.

As he pulled out the gift, I felt a coughing fit coming on, like crocodile teeth forcing their way up my throat. I had no choice but to get out of there fast.

I didn't want Adam to realise how bad my condition really is. Not then; not when he had just shown me for the first time that he could, or maybe even does, actually love me.

How can I tell him I'm dying?

It was a thought that truly rocked my soul. The Paracas may have considered Florans to be little more than animals, but we were essential animals. Those who got sick were looked after and nursed back into working condition so they could return to the stem fields. But few who were herded off to the infirmary for coughing up blood ever returned. If it's what I think it is, I'd be a fool to put in for hope. I can feel it eating me up from the inside out.

It's devouring me.

Once he had left the hut, I pulled the covers from my face and discovered it was just as I had feared. My hands were covered in hacked-up blood once again. More blood than before, pooling up in between my fingers. I frantically check the bedding to make sure I've caught it all and thankfully there's no evidence to be found on the covers.

It's radiation poisoning, I know it.

I knew instantly what it was: I'd seen it before. Back when I was a child on Flora One, I had a cousin who was about the same age as me. A sweet, sandy haired lad named Abe'L. We would play at the end of every day after our gruelling work in the stem fields, and his cheerful attitude and easy smile made life as a slave slightly more bearable.

One day we were playing tag around the Lambda barracks where Abe'L and his family lived. I remember being too fast for him and both of us giggling as he tried his hardest to catch me.

He almost had me cornered when a shadow fell over us, freezing our feet in their tracks. When we turned, a Paracas overlord stood before us flanked by two of his robotic bodyguards. Picturing the crooked smile on his face makes me shudder even now.

To our surprise the Paracas didn't yell or zap us, but instead greeted us warmly. We remained wary at first, but started to let our guard down as the alien continued showing us unusual kindness. I distinctly remember sharing a quick glance with Abe'L as we acknowledged each other's bafflement.

We were just kids. Stupid little kids.

He pulled a sweet from his tunic and said he would give it to whichever one of us was willing to help him with a small task. Abe'L managed to raise his hand before I did and was chosen for the job and I will never forget the tall, skinny humanoid leading him away.

I can still see Abe'L face as he turned to me and said: "Don't worry, Eve'E. I'll share my sweet with you."

I must have looked so upset at missing out.

That was, of course, the last time I ever saw him smile. When he returned he was never quite the same. He did get his sweet, which he dutifully shared while stonewalling all of my questions about his adventure. It was soon after he started becoming weak and withdrawn. Then he began coughing up blood and losing hair. And a week later he was dead. The beautiful boy he once was all but unrecognisable.

We discovered some time later that our slave masters were having a problem with one of their cargo vessels. There was a crack in the engine core and the access tunnel was too small for a robot or adult slave to enter. They chose to send my cousin in to seal the leak, despite the fact that it meant exposing him to lethal doses of radiation.

If I'd raised my hand a little faster, it would've been me who died that day.

Now I will die this day instead. Or maybe it'll take weeks or even months for me to meet my end. I'll wither away into a septic, unrecognisable, hairless mess. A hollowed-out monster you wouldn't want to touch let alone hold. I would laugh at the irony of it all if I wasn't so damn mad. Despite narrowly escaping death back then, it seems radiation is going to wind up killing me in the end anyway.

One night of happiness and already the Scales tip.

My current exposure must have occurred during our escape from the Preserver ship. Or perhaps it was caused by the fallout from Anne's nuclear explosion? Regardless of when it happened, it must have been significantly less radiation than what Abe'L was exposed to because it has taken three years for my first symptoms to start showing.

Could that mean I still have plenty of years ahead of me?

Do I even want to survive for a prolonged period of time with an illness of this kind? It took so long for Adam to see me as a desirable woman. Do I really want him to watch now as all my hair starts to fall out and I begin to decay? I know in my heart he would

take care of me right up until the end because that's
the kind of man he is, but I don't want to become a
burden on him. Or worse; something he pities. He's
only just started smiling again.

> *I'd rather Adam remembers me the way I am
> now than have him watch me deteriorate.*

Which only really leaves me with one option. As much
as it pains me to admit it, I need to leave him now and
never come back.

I clean my hands on the little cloth I keep secreted
away from Adam among my meagre belongings.
I can't help but notice that very little of it is now its
original colour. Emotionally exhausted, I lie still trying
to think up a plan.

XXXX

After what feels like an eternity, Adam finally goes
off to bed. I listen intently as he puts out the fire then
shuffles off to one of the neighbouring huts. And while
I had suspected he might choose to sleep elsewhere
tonight, the fact that he decided not to join me hurts
more than I care to admit.

At first I struggle to halt the sadness driving through
me, but eventually squash it with a quick reality check.
It's a good thing he's not here given the course of
action I have planned.

But I can't risk saying goodbye. I don't think I could
summon the strength to go if I actually had to face him
one last time. I'd probably end up blurting out how sick
I am and then he would never let me out of his sight.
His life would be ruined, watching me wither away.

After lying in bed another hour to make sure he's
definitely gone to bed, I get up and start packing my
things. Changing into my furs, I throw the fire lizard
skin top and bottoms Anne made me on top of my
bed. Then I scrounge up a strong length of cloth, long
enough to serve as a scarf or head wrap, and some
clean torn up rags for my moon blood.

With my meagre possessions in a pile, I fold the camel
skin blanket over them, turning it into an easy to carry
bundle. Lastly, I sling a bow and a quiver full of arrows
over my shoulder. We'd found them hidden behind
some fallen debris in one of the collapsed huts. Initially
we had practiced a lot together, but while I became
quite proficient, Adam never really got the hang of it.
He definitely won't miss them.

Picking up Adam's grey jacket from his empty cot, I
bring it up to my nose and deeply inhale the pleasant

scent of leather one last time. The memory of him handing it to me back in the Flora One habitat on the Preserver ship, as I stood there crying and naked, brings an unbidden smile to my lips. And then further sadness. It was the first of a million small acts of kindness he has done for me over the years.

As much as I'd love to take it to remember him by, I know I can't. He has so few things left from his life in the twenty-first century, it would be cruel of me to run off with one of his favourites.

I guess the necklace will have to serve as my only memento of our time together.

I pick up the necklace from where Adam placed it, then close my eyes and take a breath to summon some inner strength. I place the band around my neck and find it is nothing like the collars from my former life. I latch on to that small moment of joy, squeezing it for all it's worth.

Once the knot is firmly secured, I scoop up my sack, fling it over my other shoulder, slip on my sandals and creep silently from the hut.

As the cool night prickles the hair on my skin, I'm instantly grateful I decided to change into my warmer furs. Footprints in the sand show which of the six remaining huts Adam has decided to take refuge in for the night and even though I know I shouldn't, I can't help but tiptoe towards it. Close enough that I can hear his light snores coming from within.

I begin to cry again. Sobs so deep I fear I might wake him. It's enough to make me backpedal away from the hut and almost trip over something stuck in the sand. Looking down I see the arrow bone poking up from the sand. For a brief moment I consider pointing it in the direction I'm heading.

Don't be stupid, Eve! This is not some cry for attention! You're running away for real!

Teary-eyed, I leave the bone unmoved, then after one last look around, I walk away, off into the darkness. Leaving the village and the man I love behind forever.

Goodbye, Adam. I will never forget you.

XXXX

As the vague shapes from my former home disappear from sight, I am struck by how little I actually have planned out. Deciding I can worry about the details later, I focus first on putting as much distance between Adam and I as possible. Far enough away that I can't change my mind and go back to him.

Moving without plan or purpose under the pale light of Earth's one solitary moon, it's a good hour before I remember the leopard prints from the day before. Peering into the darkness, I realise my bow and arrows could be firewood for all the good they'd do me if I were to be attacked by one of the agile felines at night. I begin to shake. Shake like I did on that giant petal all those years ago.

I need to distract myself.

Closing my eyes, I focus on all the happy memories I created with Adam back at the village. His dumbfounded expression when I first appeared with my freshly made fishing net. The day we discovered the village and decided to make it our home. The night before, when our lips first touched. The feeling of his strong arms carrying me into the hut.

And suddenly I'm walking again. My steps soon take me to the east river, the bigger of the two, and I realise I now have an important decision to make.

Do I follow it north, south or try to cross it?

I disregard crossing almost immediately. Unlike Adam, I'm actually a strong swimmer. But regardless, the chances of reaching the other side with my sack and arrows intact are virtually nil. And I would never spot a crocodile at this time of night; I'd be serving myself up for dinner.

I could search for a craft to help me cross the rushing body of water or even build one with more time, but that would almost certainly mean encountering primitives and I'm not keen to repeat the Nile fiasco all over again.

What a terrifying experience that was!

We had been on Earth for around six months when Adam and I first found the Nile River and what we hoped might become our new home. We had looked for it for months. Adam was so excited as he had spoken at length of the famous river and how renowned it was for providing everything humans needed to survive.

It was all so different to the stem fields of Flora One, but beautiful all the same. I was shocked when we stumbled across a Lotus and Adam explained this was as big as flowers got on Earth. How I laughed at the little purple flower. But it did indeed seem like a great place to live; fresh water and plenty of wildlife and fruit to eat.

Unfortunately, we weren't the only ones who had come to that conclusion. It was only a matter of days before we encountered our first primitive; an old woman.

Running into us almost scared her to death!

Light-skinned and fair-haired, we must have seemed like monsters compared to the darker skin and hair she was used to seeing. So startled was she by our presence, that she dropped her entire basket of vegetables before running off, leaving Adam fiddling with his translator to try and open a dialogue. We ate the vegetables that night, I'm not ashamed to admit.

The next day, ten scantily clad warriors arrived with spears in hand ready to slay us. But a few warning shots from Adam's pistol got them to back off pretty quickly. They never completely let us out of their sight, however, and every attempt Adam made to try and establish communication with them failed miserably. I smile at the memory of Adam laughing when I suggested he ask the UTG to speak, "Earthling."

That was so embarrassing.

Not that Adam's attempts were much better. Every language he tried ended the same way. Either they didn't recognise what he was saying or they were flat out ignoring him.

With no way of telling the primitives we meant them no harm, we knew it would only be a matter of time before they grew bold enough to try and attack us in full force. We would never sleep soundly living near them, so that night we stole one of their canoes and paddled our way across the Nile. Then, we continued heading east to put further distance between us and their settlements.

I look back to the river racing past my toes. A canoe would be handy right about now, but without one, crossing simply isn't an option this time around. That leaves me with only two choices.

North or south?

Adam explained long ago that we had landed on the northern hemisphere of this planet. And that the further north we went from here, the colder it would get. He even told me about places on Earth where it got so cold, rain turned into a white powdery substance that blanketed the land.

He called it snow.

If it had ever snowed on Flora One, I'd not seen it. The weather on my planet was as predictable as the setting suns. But snow must have been a common sight on other worlds. Back on the ship, Adam got to visit a habitat called Krés that was completely covered in the stuff, and I was always a little jealous I didn't get to see it for myself.

It sounds so pretty.

If I go north, there is a chance – however slim – that I could actually witness this small miracle. Whereas if I head south, the only thing I'll have to look forward to is more blistering heat and windblown sand. The latter coming with the impressive ability to find its way into places it should never go.

I guess that decides it then.

So with that pitiful excuse of a plan in place, I pivot away from the rising sun and start following the river bank north.

Scales willing, I'll get to see snow with my own eyes just once before I die.

Chapter 6
EVE

It quickly becomes apparent the Great Cosmic Scales have something better to do than satisfy my curiosity regarding snow. The sun is just starting to peak over the horizon when the blockade reveals itself. Luckily, I spot the four bare-chested primitives before they see me and have ample time to get out of sight, flattening myself behind some bushes.

I had been following the river as it wound its way towards the north, keeping to its rocky shore where possible as it kept me down below the eyeline of those up in the desert proper. But it was a calculated risk. Small trees searching for water by the edge of the bank obscured my view at times and as such, I had come awfully close to walking straight into these hunters before I felt their presence.

An assortment of weapons in hand and stone daggers strapped to their waists, I watch as they gesture excitedly at what appears to be a leopard lying dead at their feet. They're right in my path. I'm going to have to take the long way around.

Curse my luck!

The oldest of the men is bald with a thick, unkept beard. I presume from the way he orders the others away from the kill, that he is their leader. I watch as he takes his axe up high above his head and decapitates the fallen creature in one fell swoop.

He then throws the head at the youngest of the group – a gangly adolescent with dark flowing hair – who promptly drops it in disgust. The other two warriors begin to laugh and jeer the boy and I instantly feel sorry for him.

The leader then takes the blood-spattered teen aside to scold him, while the other men begin preparing to skin the animal. The one with the long, black ponytail and arrows strapped to his back spreads the feline's legs, while the other one, armed with a spear, pulls the dagger from his belt and begins slicing it down the creature's middle.

The scene is anything but pretty and I quickly decide I've seen enough. I begin backing away slowly, never taking my eyes off the scary looking humans until I'm sure I'm too far away for them to hear my rapidly increasing heartbeat.

What now?

In order to give the hunters a wide enough berth to be considered comfortable, I will have to backtrack quite a distance. A journey made all the more irritating by the need to crawl over a sea of sharp stones to ensure I'm not spotted. But my options are limited, so I take a deep breath and get to it.

I've barely made it back a few metres before my toe clips a small shrub, causing it to sway unnaturally from the impact.

Have they seen me?

I freeze, my eyes darting up to the hunters ahead. But in truth, I already knew the answer. If you can take down a leopard out here, you're probably pretty good at sensing when something is watching you.

Sure enough, one of the warriors spots the tiny movement. He draws the attention of his friends to my location and I briefly wonder if they're looking at me or the bush. Imagining my head full or red curls trying to hide in a sea of green, I realise my attempts at camouflage are probably not worth a damn.

Blast it!

Leaping up, I turn and run as fast as my skinny legs will carry me. I jump over a couple of shrubs and start getting a good stride going. For a fleeting moment I even feel a bit of hope surge through me, but in truth I barely make it ten yards.

A sharp pain in my calf is followed almost instantly by all of my weight dropping to the ground faster than a wounded cloud stinger. Those large invertebrates would hover over wildflowers on Flora One trying to get to the precious pollen before the miners, but shoot an arrow through their helium-filled heads and it would drop to the floor faster than you'd think gravity would allow. In kind, I thunder into the stones and sand, the impact sending the contents of my sack spilling out across the desert floor.

As I consider the question in a daze, I wonder if I should just close my eyes and let the men kill me. This is probably better than waiting for my body to fail me one cell at a time. The thought actually gives me a sense of peace and for a moment I consider embracing it and letting fate have its way. But in that moment, I hear Adam's voice yell: "No!"

I open my eyes and search for him, but he's nowhere to be seen.

My imagination is playing tricks on me.

But the thought of his voice springs me into action. Rolling over, I discover not only am I still alive, but there is now an arrow protruding from the back of my leg. The initial shock of seeing it is quickly beaten back by the instinct to pull it out. Yet both feelings are then consumed by the sight of my attackers bearing down on my position.

I have more immediate concerns.

The pony-tailed archer reaches back to his quiver to prepare another arrow, but then awkwardly fumbles the bow. It reminds me I too have a weapon handy. With shaky fingers, I draw an arrow from my own quiver, get it nocked and ready myself to fire back. Seated in the dirt, I aim it menacingly from man to man, successfully making them rethink rushing me. The four natives slow their approach, finally coming to a stop only metres away.

Now cautious, the bald man with the bloodied stone axe barks orders at me. The other three soon start echoing similar sentiments and although I have no idea what they're saying, I can make some educated guesses. They're most likely telling me to put down my weapon or pointing out the very obvious fact that if I manage to kill one of them, the other three will be on me before I could draw another arrow.

And they're completely right, but I am not prepared to give up my only leverage just yet.

So much for dying of radiation poisoning!

I can feel warm blood seeping from the wound in my calf and my vision begins to blacken around the edges as unconsciousness threatens to take me. The fingers clutching onto the bow and its string are weakening with each breath.

If I'm going to pass out, maybe I should just fire and take my chances!

At least that'll only leave three of them to pillage my remains. I've almost convinced myself to take the risk, when a new voice calls out, startling everyone present. The woman – for the voice is clearly female – stands on the opposite bank wearing a long, black robe that obscures her features.

The oldest man with the axe yells back a warning that is full of spite and disdain. I imagine he's saying something along the lines of, "go away!" or "this does not concern you!"

But the woman refuses to let the matter drop. I'm surprised by how clearly I can hear her, despite the distance and the fuzziness in my head. The wind, too, has changed. It seems to have dropped to a waft if not disappeared completely. It's like I'm once again falling towards Earth in a translucent sphere: surreal and unnatural and beautiful all at the same time.

She's moving towards us.

Done with attempting to enforce her will through speech, the woman takes a new approach. We all watch in awe as the robed figure descends the bank and begins walking through the water. Her movement is uncanny; like a creature straight out of legend. The way the water refuses to be disrupted by her touch brings to mind something supernatural.

She reminds me of the wraith in one of father's scarier fables.

The river begins getting deeper and as it does, she slowly sinks until her head disappears completely below its surface.

What is she doing!?

The men start whispering to one another probably asking themselves that very same question. Clearly rattled by this current turn of events, they continue speaking in hushed, fearful tones. Their weapons now trained in the direction of the mysterious stranger rather than pointed at me. I suddenly realise I too have lowered my bow, so entranced am I with what is now happening in the river.

Is she trying to drown herself!?

I receive my answer moments later when her head emerges from the water's surface, bobbing up and down as she steps along the muddy bottom. She parts the water like a crocodile, without a single ripple disturbing the surface. How could I ever think something as mundane as shifting water could halt this incredible woman. She's an unstoppable force of nature, Is she an avenging angel?

Or a dark avenger?

For a brief second I consider if this being is the embodiment of the Great Cosmic Scales. Is this what my infantile mind once imagined the Scales to look like, back when I still believed them to be a person. Surely blood loss and fear are causing me to hallucinate. This is insane after all!

Maybe I died when I hit the ground, and this is all some strange afterlife.

But the throbs of pain continuing to surge up my leg are all too mortal reminders of that not being the case. Not yet, anyway.

All I can do is stare as the four men begin to lose all semblance of control. Their voices become panicked as they continue to communicate in their strange tongue. Eventually the man with the spear gives into instinct. Grunting with the exertion, he hurls his weapon with all his might in the angel's direction, and the archer, bow now back in hand, soon follows suit. Pony-tail whipping about behind him as he launches arrow after arrow in quick succession.

But the robbed being appears completely unfazed by the deadly projectiles heading her way. She slaps each one aside with no more effort than the tail of an elephant swiping at an annoying fly. It's enough for the archer to throw his weapon to the ground in disgust, or disbelief, and to begin backing away slowly.

The bald man drags himself and the skinny adolescent in front of their defeated friends and, armed with an axe and a stone dagger, prepares to attack. The younger of the two shakes like a small leaf back on Flora One under the weight of a plump sap-sucker. But as the hooded figure casually wades through the shallows, she says something to them in that same, unnervingly calm voice, which makes them rethink attacking her.

By the time she has set foot on the shore, they're weapons all lie in the dirt, abandoned. Screaming the same word over and over the four flee in terror, leaving me alone and at the mercy of this mysterious stranger.

"We must attend to that wound," the woman suddenly declares in perfect Floran.

This can't be happening!?

This is becoming too much. All of a sudden, I feel naked again, waiting under that giant petal for death to take me. Leaving Adam; getting shot in the leg; this woman. My eyes begin to blacken over again as I seek some clarity. Did this stranger just speak my native tongue? Is that even possible? How could a Floran find us on Earth? And in this era, no less! If there were Florans on Earth, wouldn't Adam have known about it? Wouldn't it have been in the books he told me about, right next to the tales of mummies and pyramids?

It takes me a full three seconds to find my voice.

"Are you Floran?" I croak nervously.

"No. I am not," comes the reply in such a fashion it's clear the sentence has no "but" coming.

With no further information forthcoming, I desperately try to rub the growing blackness out of my eyes so I can get a better look at her. With the rising sun at her back, the woman's face remains obscured by shadows and I can see nothing to help me venture a guess at her identity.

So instead I study her attire. On closer inspection her robes appear impossibly dark and despite having been dipped in the river, they remain completely dry. You'd never guess she'd been submerged in water only moments before. It's as if light and water refuse to touch her, lest they be swallowed up by the aura of dark power radiating from her body.

An uncomfortable silence fills the air as she swishes by me, kneeling in the sand to examine my spilled possessions. I stay motionless as she rummages through the limited selection, picking out my scarf. She brings it over to use on my leg and as she leans in close, I prepare to get my first good look at her face. But am quickly disappointed to discover she is wearing a mask beneath her hood.

Blast it! Who are you!?

"This is going to hurt," she informs me, yanking the arrow from my leg before I can respond.

The pain makes my vision blur worse than ever and I find myself on the verge of blacking out once again. But the robed figure uses deft fingers to tie the scarf around my wound quickly, and soon my vision begins to clear.

"W-who are you?" I finally ask through clenched teeth.

Are you the Great Cosmic Scales?

"Those men called me Tiamat, the Water Serpent," comes the answer. "I suppose that's as good a name as any."

Now that she mentions it, the golden mask she wears does make her look like a serpent. Close up, I can now make out the intricately carved fangs, forked tongue and precious yellow gems where one might expect snake eyes.

"Well thank you, Tiamat. You saved my life," I start, hoping gratitude is all this person wants in return.

"Not yet I haven't. You still appear to be dying," she replies, matter-of-factly.

Shocked by her bluntness, I clutch my newly bound leg, searching for signs that the wrapping has failed to staunch the bleeding. Was the arrow poisoned? I don't feel sick. I can't see any blood seeping out!

It still hurts like Hela!

"No. Not from your arrow wound," Tiamat explains, noting my puzzled expression. "I was referring to the radiation poisoning."

Her response hangs in the air between us, questions gathering around it like storm clouds.

How can she... do they even know what radiation is in this era?

"How could you possibly know that?" I blurt out, eyes narrowing suspiciously. "I haven't told anyone about my condition."

"Just remain calm for now. If I had wished you harm, I would have left you to your fate rather than intervening," she reminds me.

She has a point there.

"Who are you really?" I ask again.

You're not the Scales, that's for sure.

"I cannot tell you I'm afraid," but if there is any regret in her voice, I can't hear it. "What I can tell you is I am here to help."

Reaching into the folds of her cloak, she pulls out something round and red. While I can tell it's a fruit of some kind, it's not anything I've ever encountered on Earth before, or on Flora One, for that matter.

"What is it?" I inquire cautiously.

"They call it an apple. A common fruit grown in many parts of this world. This one however, is no ordinary apple. I have infused it with an organic compound I extracted from a Preserver. One bite of this and all the radiation in your body will be purged forever."

She said Preserver. I had hoped never to hear that word again. But if it were to be said, I could never have guessed to hear it here and now. By the stony banks of an Earth river in ancient times.

"You know the Preservers?" I ask, suspicion rising to the fore again.

"Yes," she admits. "You might say I have had numerous run-ins with them, but I can safely say they are no friends of mine."

I consider the fruit and the stranger's argument that killing me is not her goal. And ultimately, lying here with a hole in my leg and radiation coursing through my veins, I decide I'm not in any position to decline the gift.

I reach for the fruit and pluck it gently from her hand, holding it with all the care and reverence such a miraculous cure deserves.

Can this little thing really save my life?

I'm just about to take a bite when my mind flashes back to the Paracas slaver offering Abe'L that sweet back on Flora One and my misgivings return full force.

"You're lying," I spit the words. "I don't know anything about you. How do I know I can trust you?"

"You don't have to trust me, but do trust this. Without that apple you will die." She pauses, to let the full weight of that fact sink in. "I can assure you it will be very slow and very painful. You will wish for death many times over before you finally choke on your own blood in the not too distant future."

Tiamat, or whoever she really is, says the words not in a threatening way, but as a calm declaration of fact.

She's right. What do I really have to lose at this point? Plus, if this actually works, I can go back to Adam.

As if on cue, a cough takes me by surprise, and I heave blood onto the sand. The decision made, I take a big bite from the apple and am pleased to discover it's actually quite delicious. Chewing and swallowing the chunk, I look up into Tiamat's masked face and ask: "Now what?"

"Now we must wait," she replies simply, her Floran accent pitch perfect. "Well done, Eve'E. I knew you would see reason."

A warmth starts to spread through me, first in my stomach and then down my limbs. As it begins creeping its way up my neck, I suddenly realise she just called me Eve'E.

But I don't recall ever telling her my name.

As the warm sensation finally reaches my brain, I feel myself drifting into a deep, blissful slumber. The last thought that crosses my mind is a desperate prayer to the Great Cosmic Scales that I haven't just made a terrible mistake.

Chapter 7
ADAM X

I'd been lost in my thoughts for far too long. The realisation hits me the second my eyes finally get around to opening. Last night had been mentally exhausting and when sleep finally did come, it had been deep and dreamless. I've slept in, of that I'm certain. In fact, judging by the muggy heat in the rarely used hut, it must be around midday.

I'm punished for sitting up too quickly by a pounding headache. It feels like a railroad spike has been shoved through my temples. It takes some effort not to fall back down again. I can't help but think how good a couple of aspirins would be right about now.

Remember your promise! No more wishing for future stuff, Adam.

Before long, the doors at the back of my mind are thrown wide open, reintroducing me to yesterday's events. I feel a familiar depression washing over me. Caught between the unhappy memories of my disastrous gift to Eve and the constant throbbing inside my skull, I am suddenly grateful for the small mercy of a dreamless sleep.

I don't think I could've handled another Anne dream on top of everything else right now.

But it wasn't the necklace that kept me up last night long after Eve had sent me away. It was a burning question that continues to plague me even now.

Should I tell Eve she's a clone? Or should I keep it to myself?

Last night I wrestled with that decision for hours, staring at the bracelet on my wrist like a man possessed. I tried to think back to the moment I made the discovery about my own origins. I was exploring an area of the Preserver's ship that I shouldn't have gone to, and found my own face peering back at me through a glass tube. All but identical, except for the X.

I rub at the X for the millionth time, an ever-present reminder of the truth. As if I could ever forget it. It was rubbing the X in the dead of the night that I decided to sleep on the matter. And it's rubbing it again now that I decide I must tell her the truth, even if she ends up hating me for it.

If I'm serious about building a relationship with this woman, it has to be built on honesty.

Determined to get this over and done with before I have a chance to second guess myself, I pull on my shirt and pants before stepping out into the heat of the day. It beats down on me without mercy.

Shaking off the fog trying to envelop my brain, I march

straight over to the hut we usually share. Walking in from the bright sunlight, I'm momentarily blinded by the hut's relative darkness. With anxious energy coursing through my veins, the words begin tumbling from my mouth before my eyes have had a chance to fully adjust.

"Eve? I have something really important to tell you. I know I should have told you this a long time ago but..." I begin blurting out, only pausing once I realise her bed is empty.

Find her first and then confess, dumbass!

"Eve?!" I call out as I stumble back into the sun's scorching rays. When there's no answer, I look towards the arrow bone and find it unmoved, which is odd.

She has to be around here somewhere.

After unsuccessfully searching through some of the other huts, I head back to her bed in the hope of finding some clue. That's when I notice her blanket is also missing. The nervous energy I had moments earlier dissipates and fear takes its place. She's gone.

No! She wouldn't! Would she!?

A frantic search of the hut confirms the worst. While all of my things remain untouched, her clothes, bow, quiver and shoes are all gone.

She's run away!

She left me over a necklace? Surely not! She said it wasn't a big deal. That it just triggered some dormant post-traumatic stress craziness from a time well before I knew her.

Unsure what to do, I run out the door and in a straight line for a nearby rocky outcrop. The view from the top isn't great, but it was my best bet of spotting her shape on the horizon. I fall twice in my hurry to the vantage, shouting her name and cursing myself between yells. It's when I realise I'm crying that the fear turns to desperation. Like a butterfly climbing back into its cocoon, deep down I know it's a lost cause.

At the top of the rocks I scan in all directions and see nothing. No sign of her at all. No dust rising up from Eve's gentle steps. No leopards or other predators lurking about. Not even a scavenger bird circling a fresh kill.

Which is a good thing, at least.

It's hours before I find myself back in our hut, voice hoarse from screaming her name and looking at her empty, barren bed trying to put the pieces together.

It can't have been the necklace. Leaving over a simple misunderstanding doesn't make any sense after everything we've been through. There must have been more going on last night than I realised. There was something at the time, a feeling in my gut, that I couldn't quite place. Like I couldn't see the full picture. And I wish now I had trusted it.

Did she somehow learn the very secret I was coming over here to tell her?

It can't be that. I'm the only one on the whole planet that knows she's a clone!

Did I say something in my sleep? During one of my Anne nightmares? Did she realise how I felt about my old android companion and believe she would only ever be my second choice? Victorious by default?

Whatever the real reason, I clearly underestimated how upset she was, and, because of my negligence, Eve is now out there somewhere. Alone and possibly in danger. How will I ever be able to live with myself if something were to happen to her? Panic begins to force a fist-sized lump down my throat. It's only then that my eyes fall to the nightstand.

That wretched necklace is gone, too. She took the necklace.

The discovery hardens me like cement baking in the sun. I shake off my fears and focus all my energy on a singular goal: I need to find Eve.

Come on, Adam! What did the academy teach you about finding missing people?

I begin attacking my memories, puzzling together Adam Furst's police training and examining everything it had to offer. It's energising and gives me a sense of action and purpose. I begin searching Eve's last known location for signs of her movements.

The inside of the hut tells me very little, but outside our little home, it's a different story. While running around like a headless chicken for the last few hours hadn't done "police Adam" many favours, it wasn't long before the web of tracks began to reveal the truth.

Apart from my own heavy footprints in the sand heading back and forth between our two shacks and up the hill, I can just make out an older set of tracks heading towards the east river.

As long as the wind doesn't pick up anytime soon, these tracks should stay clear enough for me to follow!

Now charged with a single-minded determination, I secure my pistol, assemble my own little backpack of essentials and begin following her trail.

Soon I'm running and though I know such exertion of energy in this heat is unwise, I find I'm fuelled by something beyond boar, fish or pomegranates.

Is it love?

Eyes on the small footprints before me, I'm barely out of sight of the village when I round a tree and almost run smack-bang into a stranger. The near impact startles me and I trip, falling to the ground like an oaf. The shock knocks the breath from my lungs, giving me little scope to defend a blow if it comes quickly.

Where the hell did they come from!?

Panicked, I pull out my pistol as I roll back up to my feet. I aim it at the hooded figure's head as it steps past the tree.

With the sun at the stranger's back it takes a moment for my eyes to focus on the scene. It's two good breaths before I notice there is a woman cradled in the figure's arms. A woman with strawberry blonde hair. A woman I know well. A woman who is injured and unmoving. And that is when my blood begins to boil. My anger explodes like a volcano.

"What did you do to her!?" I scream with such power and rage I barely recognise my own voice.

I fire a warning shot at the tree to the figure's left, causing a shower of splinters to erupt from the trunk and crash into the dirt. The stranger is unmoved by both my demonstration of power and the menace in my voice, even as I point the weapon at their head.

God, I hope she's just unconscious.

Seeing Eve's bandaged and bloodied leg fills me with a fury I haven't felt since my encounter with a Kaa'lik drone back on the Preserver ship. When that giant insect threw Anne into a lava pit and I thought I'd lost her forever, I became so filled with unrestrained rage I shot the beast over and over again until all that remained was a twitching mass of goo.

If this hooded bastard has harmed Eve in any way, what I did to that giant bug will seem kind by comparison!

I edge closer, finger itching to pull the trigger and ask questions later.

"I did not hurt your friend," a muffled female voice says from beneath an ugly, snake-like mask.

What was that?

The words ring in my ears, rattling away the last remnants of my railroad spike headache. The thing I find most disconcerting is not the fact that I assumed it was a man effortlessly carrying this full-grown woman. It's not even the sinister looking garb and the serpent visage she wears upon her face. It's the fact that the stranger spoke those six simple words in English. A language that, in this time period, should only be known by Eve and myself.

Am I dreaming?

I laugh and can't help but notice I sound a little crazy. This is becoming too much.

Maybe I should just shoot her.

"She was attacked by a group of Sumerian hunters further up the river," she continues. "I rescued her from them and tended to her wounds. I expect she will make a full recovery, given time."

It's exactly what I wanted to hear. In fact, I'm so desperate to believe it's true, I let relief wash over me like water from a hot shower and, momentarily at least, I forget my fear and suspicion of this stranger.

All I can think of is the promise that Eve is going to be okay. I give into hope.

Focus, Adam. You don't know this woman; you don't know her true motives.

"If my intent was to hurt this woman, why would I carry her all the way back to her home?" the voice comes again, entering the space that sits empty in front of my less-than-genial look.

She may have a point, but I'm not going to be convinced that easily. I've got to keep my guard up.

"We have a hut down there you can put her in," I tell her, tilting my head to indicate its direction.

With my weapon raised and trained on my new acquaintance's back, I let her lead the way to the ramshackle huts Eve and I call home. I can't help but notice that the stranger needs little guidance.

It's almost like she knows the way already.

Once inside our humble abode, I watch as she places my small companion on her cot. I then instruct the newcomer to face the wall and keep her hands up while I take a look at Eve myself.

If this masked looney tries anything, I will kill her without pause.

But if I'm being honest, the woman probably could have cartwheeled out the door without me noticing.

That's how focused I am on Eve. Seeing her face again feels like a giant weight has suddenly been lifted from my shoulders. Guilt, fear, anger, worry; they all float away like butterflies dancing in the breeze.

I study the wound on Eve's leg. I had never been that interested in medicine growing up and I suspect Adam Furst only got through his mandatory first aid course at the academy due to some sort of clerical error. Even now I remember the curious look he gave the results of that exam. Yet from what Furst's memories can tell me, the job looks professional. Like it had been done in a hospital, rather than the middle of nowhere.

Moving my eyes over Eve's body, I notice no other significant wounds. Just a few scratches and bruises, and perhaps skin that has seen a little too much sun recently. Brushing a stray lock of curly red hair from her forehead and over her pointed ear, I lean down and plant a kiss on her soft lips.

Tasting her again and feeling the warmth of her breath on my face, an indescribable feeling pulses out from my heart and ripples through my veins.

Does this mean what I think it does?

It's only as I pull away, I notice, with some surprise, she is wearing the necklace I gave her the night before. Nestled between her breasts and close to her heart, it moves up and down with each shallow breath.

I don't know what's really going on, Eve. But whatever it is, I'm sure we can get through it.

It's clear I won't be getting the truth from Eve any time soon, so I decide to focus on the one mystery I can actually unravel right now.

"You!" I bark at the stranger, who stands as ordered with her face pressed right up against the hut's wall. "Outside! Now!"

"I do not wish you any harm," the stranger assures me as I lead her out at gunpoint. "I am here to help."

"I'll be the judge of that," I maintain, firmly, still unsure whether to treat this person as saviour or suspect.

"Surely the risk I've taken returning your friend to you is evidence enough of my good intentions," the masked woman continues.

I narrow my eyes. "For all I know, you're the one who took her in the first place and..." But even as I say the words, I realise that's not the case.

>*If it were, there would've been another set of tracks coming into the village, as well as going out again.*

"Look, if everything went down the way you say it did, you'll have my gratitude," I admit, lowering my weapon just a little so she knows I mean what I say. "But until Eve wakes up and confirms your story, I can't afford to take any chances. I hope you can understand."

"You are wise to be this cautious," comes the answer, much to my relief. "In fact, i it makes you feel any safer, you may keep your weapon trained on me while we travel together."

Travel? Travel where?

"May I suggest you grab your Universal Translation Glove," says the figure, her voice as bright as her robe is black.

How the hell does she know about my glove?

My weapon snaps back up and zeroes in on the spooky golden mask. The hairs on the back of my neck prickle and I feel my mouth go dry. What the hell is going on here? Who is this woman? She speaks perfect English and talks about things she couldn't possibly know anything about.

Is she some alien mercenary sent by the Preservers to track us down?

As she studies me through those multifaceted yellow eyes, my mind starts to race, and I feel like I'm losing control of the situation. I need to play this cool.

Don't let her get the upper hand.

"You should also bring a coat. It can get chilly where we are going," she adds.

"Whoa hold on a second there, lady," I manage, hoping she can't hear the surprise in my voice. "I haven't agreed to go anywhere with you"

"But you must," she insists. "I have come a very long way to show you something of the utmost importance."

Cocking the gun sideways, I try again. "How about you tell me who you are before we start planning a trip together, huh?"

"I cannot tell you my real name," comes the cryptic response. "But Eve and the Sumerians call me Tiamat. You may do the same if you wish."

"Uh-huh. So, Tee. Do you mind if I call you Tee?" I reply, sarcastically. "What's so gosh darn important that you had to come all this way to see little old me?"

"You would not believe me if I told you," fires back yet another cryptic response, adding to my aggravation. "That is why you must come with me Adam Ten. So you may see the truth for yourself."

She knows way too much.

"Yeah but here's the problem, Tee." I tell her. "You're giving me some major stranger danger vibes. You won't tell me who you are. And you won't tell me what you want. You're dressed like the generic bad guy from any number of eighties movies. And you know things that you couldn't possibly know unless you come from a time and a place that wasn't very kind to Eve and I. You're really not giving me a whole lot of reasons to trust you here!"

My evidence is strong, but she is unmoved. "Yet trust me you must. Your very existence may be at stake."

For a second I envisage what it would be like for a normal person to deal with this bizarre conversation. Someone who lived in this ancient ere of Earth or even someone from Adam Furst's twenty-first century. I'm sure they'd think Tiamat is a couple of french fries short of a happy meal. But I have seen so many strange things in my short lifetime and somehow, she seems to know all about them.

I'd be a fool to dismiss her outright.

"Okay then: So, let's say the stakes are really as high as you're saying," I concede after a pause. "Why hide your identity? Why don't you take off that mask as a show of good faith?"

"I would much rather not," she objects.

Her dodging my requests is starting to get really old!

"Alright, Tee. I'm done playing games here," I tell her, putting some steel in my voice. "Take off that stupid mask right now or I swear to God I will stun you and take it off myself. The choice is yours."

When she makes no move to comply, I continue: "Okay, then. I'm giving you to the count of three. One..."

I lower my aim a little so the concussive blast will strike her in the chest rather than the face.

I want her stunned, not unconscious.

"Twoooo…"

I draw out the second word hoping against hope this woman won't force me to shoot her.

Come on, lady. Don't make me do this.

"Two and a half…"

"Fine," she gives in. "It is clear we are not going to get anywhere until I take this off."

I find myself breathing a small sigh of relief. Even though the stun bolt doesn't cause any permanent damage, it is not a discomfort I want to inflict on someone who potentially saved Eve's life.

I stare at the woman as she reluctantly removes her mask, expecting to find an alien bounty hunter or something equally strange glaring back on the other side. But when I catch a glimpse of the face hiding beneath, my knees go weak. The last time I saw it, the owner was punching me in the face. The gun tumbles from my hands at the shock, dropping to the floor almost as fast as my gaping jaw.

"ANNE!?" I cry out.

It's really her!

But it couldn't be Anne. Surely this is all a dream. Anne returning is something I've wished for so many times. Yet I had given up on it ever happening and was finally ready to move on. She can't come back; not now. I mean, Eve and I... This isn't possible. It can't be happening. But it is. She's back.

That familiar voice! That prim and proper way of speaking! I should've picked up on it straight away.

How long have I been standing here staring? My eyes locked on her face and my mouth unable to form words. When it becomes clear my mind isn't going to be able to bring anything useful to the moment, Anne decides to break the silence herself.

"Hello, Adam Ten." she says, sounding as nonchalant as always.

Only Anne could return from the dead and act like she'd just returned from the shops!

"What are you doing here," I fumble. "I mean, how? I'm so sorry. I had no idea it was you!"

Embarrassed, I pick my weapon up off the ground and return it to the back of my jeans, using the movement as a chance to gather my thoughts.

A broad grin splits my face then as the enormity of the moment finally breaks through, I move in to hug her, but am brought up short when she raises a hand to stop me and steps back unexpectedly.

"Adam, while I will admit it is good to see you, I must ask that you do not touch me. I have already taken a great risk revealing myself to you and we must do everything possible to prevent making matters worse than they already are."

I stop within reach, dying to put out a hand – even a finger – and just make the contact I've longed for these past three years. It hurts pulling back, but I trust she knows what she's talking about. Anne would not ask me to keep my distance unless there was a damn good reason, so I comply. But I do want answers.

Want? I NEED answers.

"I don't understand; how are you even here right now?" I ask and with one question out the gate, the rest soon follow. "What's with all the secrecy? And why are you wearing that crazy get-up?"

"Do you remember what you were told about time paradoxes, Adam?" she returns, dodging my questions by asking one of her own.

I scratch my head as I try to recall the exact details of the conversation we had three years ago on that beach in Mersa Matruh.

"Yeah sure, I remember. You said you could get me back to the twenty-first century eventually, but we could only travel a hundred years every ten hours or so. Otherwise the risks were the same as travelling through the habitats on the Preserver ship too fast. In short, the pressure would make my head explode."

"No, what you are describing is the result of quantum pressure. I am asking what you recall about time paradoxes," she tries again, waiting patiently like a teacher trying to coax the correct answer out of a particularly dim student.

She eventually adds; "specifically, what would have happened if The Hunger had been allowed to reach the surface of Earth?"

"Oh, I remember now!" I exclaim, triumphantly. "You said if The Hunger reached Earth here in the past and ate everybody, it would alter the course of Human history. The future I know would be effectively destroyed, which means Adam Furst would never have been born and I would never have been cloned. Or in short, I would cease to exist."

"Precisely," she confirms with the hint of a nod. "It is one of those events that I am trying to prevent. If I tell you too much about what I am doing and how I came to be here, I may inadvertently cause the very paradox I am trying to prevent. Now that you know all of this, can I trust that you will not attempt to force any further information from me?"

Her eyes fall to my waistline and I instinctively tap at the gun tucked within it. With the gravity of the situation finally sinking in, I nod my assurance that I won't probe further.

"Good," she acknowledges. "Then we can proceed."

The circular mark on her head starts to glow and a slow hum begins to build. I turn my face and squeeze my eyes shut in preparation for the blinding brightness I know is to come. Only when the humming subsides do I allow myself to open them again and, as expected, I'm greeted by an all too familiar doorway made of pure light. I never realised how much I missed these portals. There is a giddy thrill in stepping through one without knowing what is waiting on the other side.

Ha! If I'm being honest, the 'what' on the other side was usually trying to eat me!

The prospect of another adventure with Anne is so enticing it makes my heart race.

So why am I hesitating?

"Anne," I sputter nervously. "I can't just go gallivanting God-knows-where with you again. Things are different now. Eve is hurt. I can't just leave her."

"Eve will be fine," she assures me without any empathy. "The regenerative compound I slipped into her food will restore her completely."

Not wanting to inadvertently cause a time paradox and contrary to my just uttered promise regarding probes and the lack thereof, I cautiously say: "Can I at least ask if you gave her nanites like you did me?"

"You may ask," she starts. "And no, I did not. I fed her an organic compound I was able to obtain that works faster than nanites do. She should be fully restored within forty-eight hours."

*Forty-eight hours? The microscopic buggers
Anne injected me with knocked me flat for
three whole days!*

"Then I definitely can't go," I reply. "If Eve can't wake up, how's she supposed to defend herself if primitives come calling? Or if a leopard wanders into the village? One did last night! This land is full of dangers."

"You need not concern yourself with time, Adam," Anne reminds me. "Regardless of how long we take I can return you to the very second of our departure. It will be as if you never left."

"This very second?" I ask, eyebrows raised in an attempt to show how serious I am.

"Yes," she confirms. Still sensing my reluctance, she adds, "what I must show you concerns Eve's future as much as it does your own."

And just like that she has me; hook, line and sinker. Anne knows me too well. I will prioritise the wellbeing of others over myself every time. I thought it was a weakness in my youth, but mum convinced me it was actually my greatest strength.

*Is Anne using that knowledge to manipulate
me now?*

A part of me is amused. How can I be angry at her? After all, I once manipulated Anne's programming to drag her into an insane adventure. It seems only fair that she's now using the same tricks on me.

I just hope it doesn't end the same way as last time. With us being separated for three years.

Grabbing my jacket, I tie it around my waist, then shove the UTG into my pocket. I also stop to check in on Eve one last time. Watching her sleep, I search my soul for that same feeling that flooded me just moments ago. But my insides are a mess; an indecipherable soup of emotional chaos not done cooking just yet.

What does Anne's return mean for Eve and I?

But I can't answer that and neither can she. Not right now, anyway. Giving her one last kiss – this time a gentle peck on the brow – I head back to the portal and jump through without further delay. And as I step through and begin to embrace the bizarre feeling of interdimensional travel once more, I'm struck by an errant thought. It enters my mind without rhyme or reason, and I can't seem to shake it.

Everything is about to go terribly wrong…

Chapter 8
EVE

What was in that apple? Had I been too trusting? Tiamat was a complete stranger and what little I did know about her made her intentions as clear as mud. Whatever chemical lay inside the fruit was clearly more than just a healing compound. Once I'd taken that first bite, the medicine – or was it really poison? – spread through my veins like wildfire. Now I could feel it working towards some unknown goal, engulfing my organs one by one.

Before I know it, my eyelids are too heavy to pry open. My body feels like it's plummeting downwards with unstoppable momentum. The sense of drowsiness is all encompassing and as I drift off, there is one revelation left bouncing around my scattered brain.

Tiamat knew my real name.

Then there is nothing. Nothing but blackness.

I should be scared. I should be panicking and assuming the worst. But there is a strange calm to be found floating in the void between wakefulness and sleep. So instead I just lay there awhile. Unconscious, but not dead. At least, I don't think I'm dead.

Slowly my mind starts returning to the land of the living, but I quickly discover my body is lagging woefully behind. Able to think, but unable to see, I strain my pointy ears in a feeble attempt to make them somehow taller and wider. Searching for any sound that might give me a clue as to where I am.

I don't hear anything.

After what seems like an eternity, I eventually find I have enough strength to open my eyes just a fraction. But as I force them open a crack, I immediately regret the motion. The light flooding into my pupils is overwhelming and even a bit painful. It takes a moment before they adjust enough for me to make any sense of my surroundings.

The first thing I notice is that I'm now naked. Again. Not a good start. The revelation strikes a chord of fear that echoes down my spine as I take in my dirty, dust covered flesh.

Why am I so filthy?

As my eyes regain full functionality, I cast my vision further afoot and spot a tree. No wait, that's not a tree. That's a stem. A flower's stem. And with that realisation my heart sinks even further. It's happening again. Just like that first day on the Preserver ship.

I'm back in the enclosure!

The shock is enough to stop me breathing. My mind starts spinning; a whirlwind of chaos and confusion. Somehow, Tiamat has put me back in the Flora One habitat. No wonder she knew my real name. No wonder she was so otherworldly and powerful. She must've been working for the Preservers all along.

I knew it was a trick!

The second she mentioned them I should have stuck with my gut instinct. How could I fall for such an obvious lie?! As I lay there ready to rage, I involuntarily suck air back into my lungs as my body forces in a long overdue breath. Then it sputters back out as a half scream, half sob.

But no cough.

Hot salty tears start streaming down my mud-smeared face and I begin praying to the Scales that my radiation poisoning has not been cured after all. At least that way my time trapped in this alien prison will be short lived.

If only I had the strength to end it all myself!

Maybe I do. The Eve I am now is a lot more resilient and a lot stronger than the Eve'E that woke up in this exact spot all those years ago. I'm not going through that again. Not after everything I've seen and done. I won't be held captive again.

But my dark thoughts are quickly interrupted when I hear a voice calling out my name.

Wait! I recognise that voice.

Shaking and still groggy, I scan the area hoping the voice I heard is real and not just the last lingering thread of sanity slipping from my grasp. Then I hear it again and am certain it's who I hoped it would be.

It's Adam! Thank the Scales!

Laughing with maniacal glee, I leap to my feet and run in the direction of his voice as fast as my wobbly legs will carry me. By the time I reach him, I'm moving so fast I almost bowl him over. As our bodies collide, I throw my arms around his neck and cling onto him for dear life. I kiss him furiously on his face and neck as I bury my tears into his flesh.

I should have known he would come for me!
He's always there when I need him!

When I feel safe enough to loosen my grip a little, I'm surprised by the amount of discomfort I can read in his body language.

Is he embarrassed because I'm nude?

I had hoped after we had finally consummated our relationship, he would be beyond letting such trivial things make him uncomfortable. But I suppose it's possible after only one time together he could still feel a little shy.

Truth be told, Adam has always been a bit of
a prude. It's one of the things I love about him.

Maybe he didn't expect to see me so soon? Or maybe he didn't want to see me at all? I did run away from him after all and without so much as an explanation.

No, if that were true, he would not be out here looking for me.

How long was I unconscious? Has he been searching for hours or days? My leg feels fine. It's in the midst of this thought that I catch the slightest bit of movement behind him.

We're not alone.

Perhaps the problem is not that I'm nude, but that I'm nude in front of a stranger. I shield my body behind Adam's bulk and peer over his shoulder, squinting into the darkness.

Who is that over there in the shadows?

I almost ask him, but then I recognise the form and that enlightenment conjures with it a host of distant and not altogether pleasant, memories. And as the person steps into the light it's puzzlement, not clarity, that follows in her wake. I know the figure waiting patiently for our embrace to end. It's Anne.

But not the beautiful, curvaceous Anne I have come to know and loathe. It's the skeletal, crystalline Anne I remember first meeting three years ago.

How can she be here!? She's dead!

I go to say as much, but when I open my mouth, all that comes out is a raspy cough. For a second I wonder if blood will follow, but the razor sharpness in my throat is gone and all that appears is spittle.

That's something at least.

Adam untangles my arms from his back and offers me his jacket without a word.

What's wrong with him?

I zip myself up and attempt to apologise for running away, but my voice has disappeared completely, leaving my mind struggling to understand where it could have gone.

It's like when we first met. Except instead of choosing not to speak, I'm physically incapable of doing so!

With that realisation, flashbacks to times I had long since buried rise to the forefront of my mind. The similarities are just too plentiful to ignore. First there's me; mute and crying in the mud. Then Adam; finding me and giving me his jacket. And lastly Anne; standing watch over the both of us like a sparkling robot sentinel. The logical conclusion?

This isn't just *like* the first day we met. This *is* the first day we met!

Have I travelled back through time as well as back to the Preserver ship!?

Making matters worse is the knowledge that not only am I unable to communicate, but I also can't seem to understand a word of what they're saying. Even though I'm fairly certain they're speaking English, a language I now speak fluently. What's happening to me? It's like my mind has been dumped in some other version of Eve that's revisiting past events.

Wait! The Universal Translator! I just need to get them to set it to Floran like last time!

Grabbing both of Adam's hands, I turn them over and examine his bare palms with annoyance.

The translation glove!? Where is it!? I'm positive he was wearing it that day!

Looking from Adam's hands to his face, I notice my odd behaviour has caused my rescuers to stop conversing. Adam's features now show open curiosity.

This must seem really strange to him.

Despite my predicament, holding his hands and gazing into his beautiful blue eyes causes my heart to flutter. Judging by the wide smile that suddenly crosses his face, I can tell he's amused by the involuntary rush of blood entering my cheeks. Knowing he noticed only serves to increase my embarrassment and makes my blush even worse.

Great! My face is probably redder than Buudaki's sun right now!

As I release his hands, Adam continues speaking with Anne and that's when I notice the missing glove is not the only difference here. There is a red bandage wrapped around his brow that wasn't there when we first met. Possibly due to some head wound I don't recall him receiving.

Funnily enough, the more I dwell on the missing UTG and Adam's new injury, the less strange the two anomalies seem. It reminds me of how even the most bizarre circumstances can feel completely normal when they're happening in a...

Dream! I'm dreaming! I can't believe I didn't realise it sooner.

It's at this point that Adam stops talking to his long-dead android companion and starts addressing me once again. I still have no idea what he's saying, of course, but the way he reaches out to me with one hand and waves with the other makes it clear he wants me to go with them.

Just like last time.

With nothing better to do until I wake up from this odd mixture of memory and fantasy, I graciously accept the offer by clasping his outstretched hand with my own.

I can only hope that when I finally do wake up, Adam will have found me for real.

Chapter 9
ADAM X

By anyone's standards, I've seen a lot in my short life. Maybe more than any other human in history. In my time on the Preserver ship I travelled to recreations of over half a dozen worlds and faced some of the deadliest creatures the galaxy has to offer. That is why I feel fairly certain I can handle anything Earth has to throw at me.

Yet despite this confidence, I still draw my weapon as soon as I've stepped through Anne's portal and arrived on the other side.

Better safe than sorry.

It takes a second for my vision to adjust and it's a long, nervous second. As it becomes clear that we're not in any immediate danger, I begin to look around in excitement, anticipating yet another strange alien world is about to explode my mind. However, where wonder hoped to stand, disappointment towers.

Did we even go anywhere?

It's a bit darker than it was before that's for certain: some time just after dusk if I had to hazard a guess.

Otherwise everything seems exactly like the location we'd just left. The abandoned village Eve and I discovered and turned into our home.

Except for that delicious smell!

Instantly my stomach responds to the odour with a growl and, like some wild beast, I sniff the air, trying to lock in on the scent. But any hope I had of indulging in the unseen feast assaulting my nostrils is ruined by a sudden onset of screaming.

Is that coming from the portal?

I squint at the shimmering gateway between here and there waiting for something to emerge. When nothing does, I try peering around its edge and only then do I find the source of such fear.

Oh boy!

A group of twenty or so men, women and children vie for position behind a fire pit hoping the flames might somehow protect them from the magic doorway that's just appeared before them. Eyes wide as saucers, they stare at the doorway of light that has just materialised at the edge of their village. Soon their attention turns to the armed man that has emerged from the portal like some sort of dishevelled god.

Think quick, Adam!

"Whoa! Okay, nobody panic! I'm not here to hurt anyone! I come in peace!" I blurt out uselessly in

English, realising only after the damage is done that they can't understand a word I'm saying.

Not quick enough!

Despite my attempts to reassure the group, it's clear I've only frightened them further. But at least the screaming has stopped. Struggling to think of a solution, I try to placate them by making some soothing hand gestures, only to realise I'm waving a gun in their faces. I quickly stuff it back into my waistband and try again.

On the plus side, I doubt any of them would recognise the gun as a threat.

One woman catches my attention. She's older than the rest and stares me dead in the eye, still as a post despite nursing a small babe on her teat.

When she opens her mouth to speak, I lean in hoping I might be able to work out the gist of what she has to say. And I do. She screeches a single word, and it clearly means "run," because complete chaos breaks out right after she says it. I'm left helpless as terrified villagers flee the light provided by the fire and portal, and disappear into the darkness beyond.

Not the response I was hoping for.

When the dust finally settles, I realise I'm not completely alone. A few brave men intent on defending their home and families stand at the edge of the village, clearly willing to do whatever it takes to stop my intrusion. Though these men have summoned enough courage to stand their ground, the way their primitive stone weapons shake in their hands makes it clear they're petrified beyond belief.

Why couldn't you guys just run like the others? Now I have no choice.

As the biggest of the men shouts something and stamps a menacing foot forward all I can do is shrug. I pull my gun back out and fire three warning shots right over their heads. Their resolve fizzles as quickly as the energy discharge from the end of the barrel. Now terrified beyond comprehension, they drop their weapons and flee into the darkness to join their family and friends.

Wonder what stories they'll tell about the strange being who suddenly appeared out of thin air and threw green lightning.

"You were not aiming at them," comes Anne's voice from behind me.

I jump in shock and involuntarily squeeze off another shot towards our hosts. The stray blast hits the fire, sending wood chips and sparks careering from the pit like fireworks lighting up the village huts. For a split-second I see numerous scantily clad butts hightailing it into the wastelands beyond.

"Jesus, don't sneak up on me like that," I tell her, calming my heartrate with a few deep breaths.

Ignoring my request, the portal vanishes in response to some unseen command from Anne and with the fire all but destroyed, there is only moonlight to hold back the encroaching darkness.

What did Anne say before scaring the crap out of me? Something about not aiming my pistol at them?

"Why would I aim at them?" I finally respond. "They were just protecting their home. Since living here in the past, I've learnt fear can work just as well as violence when dealing with primitives."

As I finish explaining my reasoning, a thick cloud somewhere high above shifts out of the way, letting a shard of celestial light shine down upon my companion's face.

She looks exactly like she does in my dream. Truly breathtaking.

"Do you think I should have stunned them?" I enquire, trying to push the intrusive thought from my mind.

"On the contrary," she replies. "I believe the way you handled them was wise indeed. In fact, I use Tiamat in much the same way you use your pistol. To persuade potential dangers to flee rather than fight."

Something in her manner suggests the statement has brought up unpleasant memories. In fact, for a second I could swear there is a tear welling up in one of her gorgeous blue eyes before she puts the golden snake mask back over her face to hide it. I quickly dismiss the thought as ridiculous. Look at me projecting emotions onto an android like a noob. It's just like the old days all over again.

I've learnt nothing.

Truth is, I'm actually kind of glad she's chosen to hide her beauty beneath that ugly mask again, whatever the reason.

I'm confused enough right now without being reminded of how unbelievably gorgeous she is every other minute.

"But I wonder; why have you not attempted to communicate with any of the primitive Humans in all this time?" she adds, any trace of sadness, perceived or otherwise, now gone.

"What do you mean? The glove doesn't work on them," I tell her, my brows knitting together in confusion.

"Of course it does," Anne retorts. "You just have to input the correct language details."

I give her a blank look. "Well, I've tried Egyptian, Arabic, Sumerian and primitive without any luck. Oh, and Earthling, how could I forget that one."

"Well of course those languages would not work. Proto Indo European would be the correct dialect for these peoples," she points out, as if it was the most obvious thing in the world.

Proto what now?

I think about the year or so I spent doing my best to form relationships with the locals only to receive death stares at best or lobbed spears at worst. I can't help but laugh, finally replying; "you know what, that one hadn't crossed my mind."

XXXX

A quick scout of the area reveals the locals are now long gone. Feeling somewhat saddened that I won't get the opportunity to explain that I'm not actually a monster, or some angry god, I settle for rebuilding the fire instead. With the flames blazing once more I eagerly turn my attention to the meal that those poor sods had left behind.

No point letting good food go to waste.

The aroma of roasting goat smells absolutely heavenly, especially given that all I've had to eat recently was a single pomegranate and a few bits of burnt fish.

As Anne and I sit by the campfire, I slowly turn the rudimentary spit and listen to my stomach groan in anticipation. Before too long I'm picking off some choice morsels of meat, blowing on them and shoving them into my mouth before they've had adequate time to cool.

Damn, that's good!

Casting my gaze over at Anne, I think of those days, long ago, when she would catch, kill and cook for me in our little cave behind that roaring waterfall. I was completely incapable of surviving in the wild without her then.

I like to think that if we went back there now, I'd be a lot more capable.

Content with watching me stuff my face, Anne takes it upon herself to answer my unasked question. She explains we've taken a short hop backwards through time, but have remained in the same location. Now that she has confirmed we are at the correct time coordinates, we are perfectly positioned to jump to this mysterious "thing" she needs to show me.

"How 'ar back did we 'ump?" I ask, trying to keep a piece of meat from burning the roof of my mouth.

"We have jumped approximately three years backwards through time," she replies, proving pig-with-his-mouth-full is one of many languages she is capable of understanding.

"No way," I say in disbelief, pointing towards the dark beyond. "Those were the guys that used to live in this village? Now I'm doubly pissed I didn't get to talk to them; I've always wanted to know why they abandoned this place and I've missed my chance to find out."

I shake my head, cursing my bad luck. "Guess now I'll never know?"

Anne sends a stare back at me that could freeze a lake and when she offers no answer to the question the mystery fades from my thoughts once more.

Wait a second, did she say three years? Does that mean...

Looking to the sky for confirmation, I find what I'm searching for almost instantly. Hanging in the dark space just above the moon and in stark contrast to stars that surround it is a single glowing orb. Something I'd recognise anywhere. A Preserver ship. Nerves flutter through my body as the gravity of this moment in time sinks in.

That means somewhere off to the west, Anne, Eve and I have just landed in Egypt. Or if we haven't yet, we will soon.

I find the thought of being in two places at once to be overwhelmingly surreal. As I struggle to wrap my head around it, I accidentally drop the meat-covered bone I was chewing on only moments earlier. It lands in the dirt with a soft thud, but I'm now too lost in thought to care for what's left of the poor goat. The other me is only hours away from experiencing the single worst moment of his life.

The landing zone in Mersa Matruh! That must be where we're heading to next!

Anne must have brought me here to save her from the explosion, it's the only explanation for how she's alive right now. Somehow, she knew. She must have sent some communication back in time to her earlier self before she detonated her nuclear battery and took down The Hunger. Why else would we come back to this exact point in time?

I'm right! I know I am!

But if Anne doesn't die, what does that mean for Eve and I? Do all the experiences we've shared these past three years get rewritten? And if they do, do we still remember everything that happened the first time around? Or is it like it never happened?

Frankly, I don't know if I'm okay with that. I don't want to forget how much I care about Eve.

Thankfully, the more I consider this scenario the more unlikely it seems. Saving Anne and suddenly having her back in our lives these past three years when she wasn't there the first time around would surely create a time paradox, not prevent one. Not to mention The Hunger might still be alive and end up eating us all.

Unless, of course, Anne's miraculous rescue of herself by herself…

Is that right?

…was kept a secret from the past me until this very moment in time. She could have brought with her a new bomb, or sabotaged The Hunger's escape pod, and then used time travel to skip forward three years. This would give Eve and I the space and time to come together unaware of her survival and before her sudden resurrection three years later. There; solved! This would prevent any alteration to history as we know it and explain why Anne is alive. Wouldn't it?

Wait, her hair.

That's right, she had short hair that night on the beach when she punched me square in the face. Right before she heroically walked out of our lives to face the galaxy's biggest threat alone and left me with nothing but nightmares. Anne's hair was still growing back after her dip in a lava pit back on Kaa'lik. Now it seems to have grown back to its original length.

Time has clearly passed for her.

Maybe she didn't jump forward. Maybe she just stayed hidden for the past three years as Tiamat. That would explain the hair, right? And why the locals have a fancy new name for her.

Argh! Time travel makes my head hurt!

The answer, I know, sits across the fire from me. Anne; watching me think it out like one might watch a child trying to tie their shoelaces.

"We're here to save you, aren't we?" I say aloud, no longer able to contain all the possibilities bouncing around inside my head.

"No. We are not," she denies, flatly.

*Well, I guess I just gave myself a headache
for nothing.*

"What the hell are we doing here then?" I ask,
exasperated by all this evasiveness.

"As I stated previously, you would not believe me if I
told you," comes the stubborn response. "Or you would
take it the wrong way, which also does not benefit our
current situation. When you are ready, we can proceed
to Scotland where I will show you the truth."

*Scotland!? Why the hell would we need to go
all the way up there?*

Anne glances down to the chunk of goat now cooling
rapidly on the ground, already covered in sand and
ants, then back up to my eyes. "Can I assume you are
finished eating?"

"What, now?" I query. "Don't you need to recharge your
portal-making batteries – or whatever it is you use to
pull off that trick – for, like, another half a day?

Anne pauses for the briefest of seconds and it occurs
to me I've never seen her do that before. She's always
seemed to know her response before I've even
finished the question. But a response does indeed
come my way.

"Previously I've partitioned a significant portion of my
power inside an emergency backup battery in case

we run into danger on the other side of the jump. This will ensure I have the ability to act in our defence if required. In this instance, I know exactly what is on the other side and such a development is not likely. So I can redirect the energy into my portal generator and enable a quicker jump."

Really? But what about the time…

"Plus, I'm expecting company shortly," she adds. "Those villagers will likely return."

I shrug away my worries and look down at the fire, crackling at the night air. As much as I would enjoy staying in the village and gorging myself further, my curiosity now far outweighs my hunger. Wiping greasy fingers on my pants and leaving the rest of my meal for the scavengers, I get up in preparation for the final leg of our journey.

"Fine, let's get going then," I grumble. "All this suspense is killing me."

Anne stands without a word and opens a new portal, bringing a blinding light to the darkness once more. I cast a look over the village and let the warmth in the air grace my skin one last time as Anne waits patiently.

I'm about to jump into the light when something in the goat meat resting at my feet grabs my eye. I pick it up and run my fingers over it to clear off the sandy chunks still clinging onto the bone beneath. It's a familiar shaped bone, so I place it in the sand and point it towards the portal.

"Force of habit," I tell Anne, and when she fails to react, I shrug and step through.

XXXX

Anne was right about one thing, Scotland is chilly. As we arrive, I'm immediately grateful she suggested I bring a jacket when we first began our journey. Untying it from my waist, I slip it on, then pull the zipper up as high as it will go. Right up until it begins to pinch at the flesh under my chin.

At least it's not as cold as Krés.

Pistol once again at the ready, I take a quick look around and get the lay of the land, starting this time with the space directly behind the portal.

Nope, there's no village full of kilted Scots to freak out.

Travelling through the portal has turned night into day once more. I blink up at the sky attempting to locate the Preserver ship somewhere up in the heavens. However, the dark grey clouds now covering the sky makes that impossible.

Instead, I turn my attention to the surrounding land. I'm standing at the point where the base of a hill meets a rocky coastline; where land meets sea. On one side, a beautiful blanket of green stretches off as far as the eye can see. On the other, waves mercilessly thunder against a shore of jagged black stones. Their rhythmic crashing the only sound outside my own footsteps.

My eyes draw a line up from the waves across the churning ocean towards the darker clouds looming up on the horizon. As I do so, I take in a freezing lung full of cold air and watch it become steam as it leaves my body a heartbeat later.

Looks like a storm's coming.

Anne joins me on the scenic hillside and the doorway of light promptly closes behind her. I gesture out at the open expanse where there appears to be no human presence at all. Or anything else of note, really.

"Well Anne, you're the tour guide. Where to next?" I ask impatiently.

"It should be just over that rise," she tells me, pointing to the nearest hilltop.

For a moment I consider pointing out that she could have just opened the portal at the top of the hill and saved us the effort of climbing up, but realise there is nothing to be gained from the rebuke. So instead I take a deep breath, brace my thighs for the coming pain and begin climbing the lazy incline. A number of laboured breaths later, we've reached the crest and I'm bent over hands on knees. Anne stands there unaffected, rubbing it in.

At least she could pretend to be puffed.

Eventually I stand and swing my eyes across the vista. From my new vantage I can see the land rising and falling in all directions. But ultimately, no matter which way you look, the green always gives way to blue.

Are we on an island?

"I thought you said we were in super sunny Scotland?" I voice my confusion.

"We are," she answers. "Specifically, the island of Papa Westray in Northern Scotland."

Thankful once again for the jacket, I continue to push: "Uh-huh. You wanna explain why you brought me to this miserable place?"

"The reason is right there," she replies, pointing to a burrow-like opening about two-thirds up the next hillside. I hadn't even noticed it at first among the mist, but there's no doubting what it suggests.

Someone lives here.

As we make our way toward it, it becomes doubly clear the cavern is not a natural formation, or even something dug out by the local wildlife. Assuming there is local wildlife here, that is. The flat slabs of rock bordering the rectangular opening are positive proof of Human habitation.

Or humanoid habitation at the very least.

"Is someone in there?" I ask.

"Yes," Anne confirms. "There is a human male I wish you to meet."

As we approach the entrance, Anne calls out in a loud voice: "Brien!?"

Who the hell is Brien!?

I hear shuffling inside and soon a short man with a shock of red hair and a thick beard emerges. He spots Anne first, who is still draped in her dark Tiamat disguise, and gives her a gap-toothed grin of recognition. Then he turns his gaze on me, looking me up and down with something akin to curiosity.

"Adam," Tiamat announces without fanfare. "I would like you to meet Brien."

Chapter 10
ADAM X

After Anne introduces me to Brien, the stocky man in the dirty brown vest and pants waves us indoors without further word. Just in time, too. I feel the first droplets of rain begin to fall from the heavens as I duck down to avoid bumping my head on the low stones that border his entrance.

Ew, what's that smell?

Before my eyes have even had a chance to adjust, I find my nose wrinkling involuntarily due to an unpleasant odour. Worried the reaction might insult the owner of this curious little abode, I make a concerted effort to ignore the pungent aroma. Keeping my face as straight as humanly possible, I turn my attention instead to the dimly lit chamber. Brien's home.

Wow!

I have to admit to being impressed. Smell aside, the intricate stonework I noted around the doorway is even more elaborate within. Brien's entire domicile is one circular room completely lined on all sides by stones hand cut into something akin to bricks. What's truly impressive though are the way the grey stones have been fitted together so perfectly. The mismatched slabs of rock interlocked so precisely they don't even seem to require mortar.

It must have taken him ages to dig all this out and gather all this stone.

As I step further into the home the wall on one side opens up. An optical illusion created by the laying of the bricks had hidden a hallway from me at first. As I look into it I can see another room much like this one at the end. Although it's packed with an array of farming style tools.

I wonder what this guy could accomplish if he had a laser level and a good wet saw?

I look up towards the roof and again can only marvel at the engineering. Everything in its design must be so on point or that arched roof would never be able to hold back the weight of the dirt above. The room isn't tall; but neither is Brien. And by my estimate, the ceiling can't be too far off the top of the hill anyway.

I'm surprised it wasn't showing from the outside in truth.

Turning back towards the warming embrace of the main room, I continue my tour. Despite the cold outside, the ancient abode is surprisingly warm. Our host wastes no time removing his vest and dropping it on the dirty floor. Everywhere I turn I see an assortment of knick-knacks and tools making it clear Brien is a man who likes to tinker.

It's also clear that Brien is a man in need of a garage sale!

Vegetables, which must be grown elsewhere on the island, lay strewn across a big stone table, besides which a chair and a simple, yet perfectly carved canoe, balance against the curved wall. The vessel looks well-used, too. For fishing perhaps?

Or maybe this is how he reached this desolate location in the first place.

Towards the back of the burrow, I can just make out a straw bed and… what the hell is that?

Is that an indoor pigsty?!

It is! I now realise what's responsible for the funky smell I picked up when I first entered. Cordoned off inside a pen, three fat pigs begin to oink noisily as they wallow in their own filth.

A thought from somewhere deep inside my memory-stamped brain suddenly shoves its way to the front of mind. It's a recollection of original Adam's mum standing in his bedroom yelling, "this room is a pigsty!"

The fallacy of that moment makes me chuckle and this causes Brien to give me a strange look. Does he think I'm laughing at his home?

Another great first impression to add to the list Adam, well done.

Thankfully, Anne takes control of the situation before things get too awkward. She begins busily conversing with Brien in his native tongue, while he nods enthusiastically in response to every word she says. Unable to understand any of it myself, I decide now is as good a time to put my translator to use. I pull the black glove from my pocket and try to slip it over my left hand without anyone noticing.

Tapping it twice brings its small green screen to life. I bring it right up close to my lips and whisper: "Proto Indo European."

In complete disregard of my attempts at remaining in stealth mode, a spirited chirp of acknowledgement erupts from the device.

> *Shut up you stupid glove!*

Responding to the alien sound, Brien glances in my direction, but quickly dismisses it as less important than whatever Anne is saying. I manage to get the UTG volume down to a reasonable level before it can spit out too many words.

> *He already thinks I'm laughing at him. He doesn't need to know I'm eavesdropping on him as well.*

Listening in, I hear nothing along the lines of inter-dimensional, spacefaring or time-hopping. Nor do I learn anything that explains why I've been brought to this strange place. All I hear is Anne providing tips on proper pig rearing and the best way to harvest crops. Not exactly what I would consider important information. Still, Brien seems overjoyed to see her scary, masked face, that much is clear. Although he stays tight-lipped throughout her lecture.

It's almost like he worships her.

That suspicion is quickly confirmed when I hear Anne refer to herself as the Divine Goddess, Danu. At that my ears prick up like a prairie dog catching a scent. Yet another fake name to add to her rapidly growing list of aliases.

How does she keep coming up with all these bizarre names? And why hasn't Brien said a word in reply since we got here?

Now curious to hear the man speak, I step towards them with a prepared greeting in mind. Unfortunately, before I can interject myself into their conversation Anne shoots me down.

"Sit down and remain silent!" she orders so abruptly it makes me flinch.

The cordial words I had prepared now forgotten all I can do is sigh. The UTG's screen flashing once in response to my noisy exhalation as if warming up to talk, before realising the sound is not something in need of translating.

It appears I've angered the great and powerful Danu.

Cranky at being dismissed in such a rude manner, I'm about to openly curse my android companion before remembering my earlier promise that I would follow her lead without question.

I'm sure she has a good reason for wanting me to keep my trap shut, but does she have to be such a bitch about it?

Stepping back, I absentmindedly begin toying with my bracelet and listening to Anne continue making mindless small talk. Eventually, I start to wander around again, peeking about the hovel hoping it isn't too offensive to my host.

I soon find the source of the warmth: a fire secreted away in a hearth that has somehow been engineered right into one of the walls. It's hard to work out how the weight of the wall above doesn't crush the recess. Again, the workmanship is absolutely stunning. A pot of stew slowly warms over the heat and in this spot the delicious smell of dinner wins the battle against the odour billowing out from Brien's animal roommates. I sit down on a nearby stool and stir the contents, losing track of the conversation behind me as my mind evaporates into the bubbles on the stew's surface.

By the time the contents of the pot start to boil in earnest, a combination of boredom and irritation has really begun to set in. I begin dwelling on my earlier misgivings regarding this trip.

Well this is some adventure.

Did she seriously bring me all this way to watch her
talk shop with Brien the pig farmer? Is this even
the same Anne I knew and loved? All these aliases
and weird relationships with people from the past.
I think back to the last time I saw her: a blinding
light exploding in the distance. And then I start to
wonder if surviving a nuclear explosion has somehow
scrambled her circuits.

There's no doubting it. Something about Anne has felt
a little off ever since she got back. Not that I can put
my finger on what the problem is, exactly.

Is it all the evasiveness and secrecy?

No, that can't be it. Anne being secretive is nothing
new. In fact, deceiving me was literally a part of
her original programming back when I first met her.
Her primary mission was to keep me alive, but her
secondary function was to convince me that the
artificial habitat we were sharing was really Earth.

*As long as she could do so without
endangering my life, of course.*

That's why for our first two weeks together, she
pretended to be an ordinary Human woman. Ordinary
mute Human woman, at least. With the strength to
fling a wild boar over her shoulders like it was a silk
scarf. Actually, now that I think about it, even after I
forced her into being honest by pretending I was going
to harm myself, she still chose to keep the fact I was a
clone to herself.

Perhaps it's the weird cosplay thing she's got going on that has me spooked?

No, that's not really new either. Even while we were trying to escape from the Preserver's alien zoo, Anne seemed to display a penchant for playing dress-up. First, there were the fur loincloths she made for the two of us. Then the rubbery, shell-encrusted Kréken armour she scavenged from Zanatos' predecessor.

I still feel bad that that poor clone had to die over a simple misunderstanding.

When we got to the ship's core, Anne found the clothing Adam Furst was wearing when he was abducted and liberated a nondescript black bodysuit for herself. And when her new skin-tight number got burnt to cinders in the Kaa'lik enclosure, she fashioned herself and Eve leather sarongs using skin from a decapitated fire lizard's head.

She's always dressed weirdly. So, if it's not the secrecy or her questionable fashion choices, what is it?

I'm pulled back to the here and now when Brien's arm comes rushing past my face wrapped in a cloth. The pot of stew is bubbling up and overflowing into the fire and, lost in thought as I was, I completely failed to notice. As Brien lifts it from its fiery hell, he throws me yet another look, this one much easier to translate.

He must think I'm a complete idiot and I can't say I really blame him.

Making my way back to the little stone table and taking a seat, a stew-filled bowl and long wooden paddle is placed before me.

This actually smells pretty good!

Conscious of Anne's instructions to stay silent, I look to Brien and give him an affable nod in acknowledgement of his culinary talents.

The gesture unfurrows Brien's brow and seems to undo a fraction of the terrible impression I've made thus far. After preparing two additional bowls, he gives me another one of his gap-toothed grins, then shocks the hell out of me by grabbing his crotch and fumbling with the knot on his pants. I sit stunned as he drops his drawers to the ground…

Is this guy coming on to me!?

…then proceeds to stroll outside stark naked. I throw a frazzled look at the doorway, sending a silent question at the man's backside as it disappears into the rain.

"Brien needs to go to the toilet," Anne explains.

When you've got to go, you've got to go.

Not wanting to talk to Anne after the way she dismissed me earlier, I stare into my bowl of soup awaiting Brien's return. In my peripheral vision I can see Anne's masked face turn in my direction, but as annoyed as I am I refuse to give her the satisfaction of looking back.

Arms crossed over my chest like a petulant child, I continue to stare blankly at my food until, eventually, she positions herself directly across from me and I'm forced to look up and meet her gaze.

"You are upset with me," she states redundantly, as if my actions hadn't made that fact abundantly clear.

"Oh, now you want to talk?" I finally respond, bitterly.

"I apologise if my earlier remarks offended you," Anne offers. "Brien is under the mistaken impression that I am a goddess and that you are my manservant. A little arrogance on my part seemed necessary in order to maintain the charade. Can you forgive me?"

Her words take me back to a time when she pretended to be the servant and made out that I was the master. The ruse was done in order to convince Zanatos that I was a great warrior, which I learned was necessary when one wishes to converse with a Kréken. And thanks to her understanding of alien etiquette, Zanatos and I were able to become the best of friends.

Or kin, as Zee liked to say.

Remembering how effortlessly she fell into the role of the servant that time around, I realise I really shouldn't have a problem doing the same on this occasion.

"Okay, that kinda makes sense now that you've explained it," I admit. "I officially forgive you, oh wise and powerful Danu."

"Just Danu will suffice for the time being," she says.

Well thank Danu for that.

With too many questions to ask, I let the matter drop, pick up my paddle and sample some of the stew. It's as excellent as its smell had indicated. "So, now that that's sorted, just Danu, I was wondering; what's Brien's deal?"

"His deal?" Anne volleys back in a manner that all but confirms this is the same companion I risked my life with all those years ago.

"Him not speaking," I elaborate.

"I am afraid Brien is incapable of speech," Anne explains to my surprise. "When he was a child his father cut out his tongue."

A mouthful of stew spits out across the table as I fail to contain my shock.

"Are you serious!?" I exclaim, horrified by both the answer and the calm way in which it was delivered. "How could someone do that to their own kid!?"

"I believe he used a sharp cutting implement of some kind," Anne adds.

"Well I figured that much out!" I throw back, still stunned. "What I meant was, why would a father do that to his own son!?"

"Growing up," Anne reveals, "Brien and his mother were beaten by him on a fairly regular basis. During one of these beatings, young Brien summoned the courage to voice his objection to the manner in which they were being treated. His father decided cutting out the boy's tongue was a reasonable punishment for daring to speak back to him in such a manner."

"That's messed up!" I state, feeling nauseous as I imagine the psychological scars that must leave on such a small child.

"I agree," responds Anne, and for a second I can't help but wonder if that's an emotionally driven response or typical android detachment.

Maybe she has changed?

"Brien's love for his mother was the only reason he remained in such an abusive environment," Anne continues. "When she eventually passed, he left the mainland and his father behind forever."

"He built himself a small seafaring vessel," she continues, pointing towards the canoe I noticed earlier leaning against the wall, "then set out to sea where, as luck would have it, he stumbled across this small island. He has remained here ever since, content to live out the remainder of his life farming pigs and growing vegetables."

"Wow," I sigh, unable to comprehend Brien's journey. "So, how did you guys meet?"

"I first met Brien long ago and always found him to be a rather intelligent individual," Anne reveals. "At least in comparison to the other humans who live in this era. That is why I check in on him every five years."

"Every five years!?" I repeat much louder than I had anticipated, flabbergasted by the thought.

How long has she been living without me?

Before I can ask her, the steady pitter-patter of rain is suddenly drowned out by what sounds suspiciously like an incoming jumbo jet. A jumbo jet set to land right on top of us. I jump to my feet in shock and stare up at the ceiling as if it's about to come crumbling down.

"WHAT'S HAPPENING!?" I scream over the sound. But unfortunately, I can barely hear my own words let alone anything Anne might be trying to convey.

As the ground begins to tremble, small clumps of dirt begin falling from the ceiling and my initial thoughts on its engineering begin to come into question. Not wanting to end up buried alive, I run outside only to be immediately assaulted by the elements. Rain and high winds cause my hair to whip about wildly, but that's the least of my problems. Bright beams of light crisscross the evening sky, cutting through the dark, grey gloom.

Is it the Preservers!? Have they finally come back for me!?

Squinting up at the craft's brightly lit underside, I realise that if this is a Preserver ship, it's unlike any

I've seen before. This vessel is triangular in shape and has powerful spotlights built into each of its sharply angled points. They seem to be scanning the surrounding hill as the craft slowly descends. Just before it lands, the three beams seem to converge on a fixed location moments before the craft disappears from view over the rise that crowns Brien's home.

Wait a minute! Where's?...

"BRIEN!?" I yell all too loudly now that the roar of the alien spacecraft's engine has diminished.

"That is a long-range scout ship and I detect one Paracas life sign on board," Anne informs me. "I recommend caution!"

Paracas!? As in the evil alien drug traffickers that enslaved Eve's people!?

That realisation finds embers of hate in the pit of my stomach and stokes them into a raging fire. I scramble up the slippery hillside in search of our naked host. And as I reach the hilltop, I draw my weapon in preparation for a fight. Now standing on what is essentially Brien's roof, I am finally able to see the vessel clearly for the first time.

From my new vantage I notice that, unlike the flat underside, the top of the craft appears curved with a small reflective bubble built into its top. It's just like something you would expect to see in a 1950s middle-American creature feature.

That's gotta be the cockpit!

As water droplets slide along the ship's dark surface and cascade over the sides, my eyes are drawn to the landing struts that now protrude from beneath the vessel. Also, underneath the craft are the searchlights I saw earlier, except now they appear trained on a solitary figure who is suspended in mid-air at the point where all three beams converge.

"Hold on, Brien! I'm coming!" I call out, as I rush down the slope to free him from their gravity defying hold.

In my haste, I lose my footing and end up rolling like two cats in a fight all the way to the bottom, completely saturating myself in the process.

Some hero I am!

I don't even bother trying to get back to my feet. Instead, I roll up to a knee, take aim, and fire three shots in quick succession. Each of my blasts take out a tractor beam, which results in Brien dropping like a falling branch into the soaked earth.

"Go! Get out of here!" I order, my words echoed a second later by the UTG.

Wide-eyed and terrified by his near abduction, Brien is more than happy to comply with my instructions. He runs past me without a second look, his privates slapping against his thighs as he scrambles madly up the hillside and back to his goddess.

Speaking of his goddess, where the hell has Anne disappeared to!?

Finally taking the time to lift myself from the wet grass, I'm barely back on my feet when a hiss of pressurised air draws my attention to a circular access port in the ship's belly. That's when an enormous humanoid – presumably the pilot – jumps out, landing in the mud with a splash and immediately swinging its massive rifle in my direction.

Holy crap!

Before I can even call out Anne's name, a barrage of sizzling plasma volleys in my direction, threatening to end my existence forever. In that moment, only one thought comes to mind.

Danu was absolutely right! I should've exercised caution...

Chapter 11
EVE

Holding Adam's hand as he leads his deceased android companion and I deeper into this most bizarre of dreams, I begin to wonder if I actually want to wake up. Each molecule of my skin reaches out to the rough calluses on his palm in the hope I can bring our touch even just a micron closer. Perhaps I could stay in this dream with him forever?

Where death cannot touch us.

But dreams never play by the rules. Upon seeing Adam's little Flora One camp, he let's go of my hand and walks on alone, leaving me to shuffle the last metres in Anne's shadow as she follows close behind.

It's not long before I realise my dream is once again resuming a familiar path. The damp clearing is exactly the way I remember it. The makeshift tent, created from a giant queenspire petal, still occupies the centre of a small clearing.

I'm so deep in reminiscing about how kind Adam was in those initial moments, that I start to frown before I realise why. From memory this doesn't end well. This peaceful moment is going to change very soon.

Danger is coming.

Armed with foreknowledge of what's to come, I decide to conduct myself differently than I did the first time around. Instead of cowering inside the tent like a frightened skitter-bug, I remain on guard, ready to make my move when everything goes to Hela.

I wish I had some way of warning them!

If events continue as they did previously, and I have no reason to believe they won't, a fire lizard attack is imminent and all I can do is sit around waiting for it to happen. I could run off on my own, of course. But even in a dream, I can't bring myself to leave Adam at the mercy of some monster.

Besides, we outran it once! There's no reason we can't do it again!

So I wait. My eyes dart about anxiously in search of the threat I know is coming. The jerky movements of my head make the red curls of my hair sway like flowers in the wind and each time a strand brushes past a shoulder it's all I can do to keep from jumping out of my skin. Jaw clenched tight, I pace back and forth waiting for the inevitable. Then finally, just as I had predicted, I hear a deafening crash.

It's landed! We need to go, now!

Adam's eyes widen as he turns his head towards the disturbance. Thick, trunk-like stems begin parting as the winged reptile pushes them aside with frightening ease. The ground trembles with each step as the enormous beast draws ever closer. The memory of our last encounter is so vivid I can already smell its putrid breath before it has even reached us.

The smell of death.

Adam freezes in fear and I tug at his arm to snap him out of it. Once I have his attention and his gaze locks to mine, I silently plead with him to run.

Come on! We need to go! Now!

Fortunately, he doesn't require much convincing. The terrifying cacophony of sound is enough to compel even the bravest person to flee and soon the three of us are bolting through the forest as fast as our legs will carry us.

XXXX

Before long, Anne – her tireless mechanical legs giving her an unbeatable advantage – takes the lead. Adam follows close behind, dragging me along in his wake as I desperately try to match his long strides and her inhuman gait. Running for our lives, Adam's hand pulls at mine as we dodge and weave through the undergrowth. And behind us, the scaly behemoth roars in frustration as it attempts to navigate its massive bulk between the thickening stems.

As we make our mad dash, Adam asks Anne a
breathless question I can't quite hear. But if memory
serves, it's something along the lines of, "how much
longer until you can open a portal?"

To which I recall her replying she needs a few more
minutes. The memory sends a sudden wave of relief
through my body.

We make it. I've been through this before. I know
we will soon leap safely into the next habitat on
the Presevers' ship; slightly singed, but otherwise
unscathed. In fact, I realise I can already hear the
rhythmic pounding of the fire lizard's heavy footsteps
falling further behind as we weave through the forest
of stems.

A smile begins to creep across my face and I almost
start giggling. I relax my gait as stress lifts from
my body and I glance towards the blue sky that
occasionally peeks through the petals above. And it's
then, feeling way too cocky, that the Great Cosmic
Scales decide to swing against me once more.

My foot catches on an upraised root and my grip on
Adam's hand slips as I go tumbling to the ground. A
shriek of pain exploding from my lips as I face plant

into the dirt. The stress that had left me moments before falls back down on my back like a boulder dropped from the top of a cliff.

> *Blast it! How could I have forgotten this part!? I'm such an idiot!*

Without any thought for his own safety, Adam turns back and instantly begins lifting me back up. Unfortunately, I know I've twisted my ankle even before I'm back on my feet.

> *It hurt for months!*

In the short time it takes for all of this to transpire, our pursuer closes the distance between us. I lift my eyes up in the direction of death. A snout full of needle-sharp teeth hanging below beady orange eyes burst through the undergrowth. Saliva drips from its wide mouth and that smell once again envelopes us like a cloud of rotten gas.

> *Don't panic! It won't reach us!*

Despite my faith, I squeeze my eyes shut in the hope I might blink the last of this dream away. It's then that I feel Adam swing me away from danger, using his own body as a shield. The movement is violent.

> *He's stronger than he realises.*

Snap! I hear the fire lizard's mighty jaws slam shut so close to my face pieces of enamel splinter off and settle into my hair, propelled forward by its foul breath.

Even though I knew it would fall a few inches short of the mark, the moment is still terrifying. I find my heart is beating so hard it feels like it could burst from my chest and race off on its own.

I forgot how terrifying this all was!

I open my eyes one at a time to confirm the scene matches my memories. And like before, the beast's wide body has become wedged between two of the thickest stems I've ever seen, leaving it perilously close, but ultimately short of its Floran snack.

That's strange, I don't remember being covered in saliva last time.

Wiping my face with my forearm, I try to brush off the icky substance before it pools into my eyes and I'm shocked as my skin comes away red from the effort.

Why is it red?

I can feel my eyes widen, reaching out for clarity. My mind begins to tumble in on itself in shock, slowing time down to a crawl. Seconds into minutes. Minutes into hours.

Did it get me?

I look down and see red all over me. Blood. It's a horror show. A gasp manages to escape my mouth as I try to stand, only for my ankle to give way, sending me back down to the mud. The lizard chews at something in its mouth momentarily, it's teeth also painted red. I feel something shift on my left shoulder and turn my head to see Adam's hand.

No!

Adam is on a knee beside me, one hand on my shoulder as he shields me, his other raised out towards the fire lizard as if to halt it in its tracks. Only his other hand is gone.

No! No! No!

The beast's teeth had clamped down on Adam's outstretched arm. Everything from his left elbow onward is severed as a result. The sight is gruesome, with bone and muscle left dangling like shredded leaves.

No! That wasn't supposed to happen!

Through his remaining hand, I feel Adam's body start to tremble as he goes into shock. The lizard roars again and I realise it wants more than that small snack. Adrenalin suddenly fires through me and time restarts. I jump back to my feet, screaming through the pain. I throw Adam's remaining arm around my waist and help him stumble away as the fire lizard, in its rage, tries to break free from its trap. Unfortunately, my twisted ankle means our progress is painfully slow.

Where's Anne!?

She's abandoned us that bitch. And that fire lizard isn't about to give up. It's got two easy meals right in front

of it and now that it's had a taste nothing will stop it.
When the stems fail to budge, the monstrous creature
tries a new approach. The sound of its deep inhalation
could only mean one thing.

It's going to burn us alive!

At the pace we're moving, I realise there's no hope of
avoiding the gout of flame that will soon come. I look
back as the beast's nostrils flare; its eyes piercing
my soul. It opens its mouth and a tornado of orange
billows out in our direction. I hug Adam close, burying
my face in his trembling chest so deeply I almost don't
notice the dark shadow that steps from the stems and
fractures the oncoming light.

It's Anne. She comes out of nowhere, stepping her
nearly indestructible frame between the mega lizard
and her charge just in the nick of time. Flames lick
around her, hot enough to scorch my exposed skin,
but weakened considerably.

Thwarted, the predator howls in frustration, before
belching fire in our direction once again. And again,
the android's superhuman frame takes the brunt of the
blast without buckling.

That was way too close!

Determined not to be outdone, the lizard returns its
attention to the stems preventing its movement and
struggles with renewed vigour. The immediate crisis
now averted, Anne picks us both up like pollen sacks,
throwing one of us over each of her shoulders.

Now forced to carry two dead weights, Anne's previous speed is greatly reduced. Dangling helplessly over her back, I watch in terror as the fire lizard finally rips through the stems that hold it back. It turns its menacing head in our direction and picks up the chase. It gains ground quickly this time.

We're not going to make it!

A ten-metre gap quickly becomes five, which quickly becomes three. I hear the reassuring sound of Anne's portal opening, but the fire lizard is right on us now. I look over to Adam trying to find his eyes one last time. To say what needs to be said.

I'm sorry.

But he's unconscious, his head slamming hard against Anne's exposed crystalline form. His mauled arm a gruesome mess.

This is no dream! It's a nightmare!

I feel the hot breath of death on me once again and raise my head in defiance. And the last thing I see as we cross the threshold is the hungry reptile preparing for one final lunge, the charred pieces of Adam's missing arm still wedged between its crooked teeth.

Chapter 12
ADAM X

I've had a lot to take in over a very short amount of time. One minute I'm watching a man's bare bum scurry up a hill. The next, there's a large armoured alien trying to fire a plasma beam through my brain.

It's a Paracas and that thought alone is enough to fill me with dread. Knowing what these intergalactic slave traders did to Eve and her people, I have no doubt this creature is my enemy. Even if I didn't know their history, the fact that it's using a plasma rifle to blast me out of existence would've been a dead giveaway.

The whole scenario is such a shock, it doesn't even occur to me to shoot back until long after my foe has begun firing in my direction. Luckily, with the rain and the wind taking control of the battlefield, I escape the initial volley unharmed.

That was lucky.

Desperately scrambling for cover, I manage to stay one step ahead of the deadly beam of blue energy as it licks at my heels. Finally, I find refuge behind one of the ship's landing struts.

Now unable to hit me without damaging its own vessel, my attacker hesitates, releasing the trigger and ending the barrage of plasma. Even at this distance I can hear the weapon hiss in relief and now that it has stopped firing, the sound of rainfall returns. It's in that split second, I seize my opportunity and return fire. Before my adversary has had a chance to seek cover of its own, I lean out and put one well-placed stun bolt right into the alien's chest plate.

Electricity dances over his rich, red body armour, causing it to momentarily spasm before going rigid and toppling backwards. My extraterrestrial foe hits the ground with a loud "thunk."

Well, that was easy!

To be fair, I highly doubt this Earth invader would have experienced anything more than sticks and stones flying back in its direction during previous jaunts. The weapon I'm packing won't exist on this planet for thousands of years.

If at all.

I eyeball the gun in my hand with newfound appreciation. I've had to lean on it more than I would care to admit over the last few years. Without it I may never have made it this far.

Now that the danger has passed, I double tap my Universal Translation Glove and say, "Paracas," before cautiously approaching my felled opponent.

My weapon still trained on the alien's unmoving form, I kick his plasma rifle out of reach and hear it clatter across the wet grass. I then attempt to communicate with my conquered foe.

"Hey, big fella. You awake in there?" I ask, in as soothing a tone as I can muster.

Not that I can be sure the many nuances of human speech can manifest through the UTG's detached, computerised translation.

The bulky creature remains silent and still.

"I didn't wanna shoot you," I assure the beast, hoping I can still de-escalate this situation. "But you didn't really leave me much of a choice now, did ya?"

The blue, V-shaped visor covering its face flickers sporadically, but otherwise, there is no answer.

Did I accidentally kill the Paracas? Where the hell is Anne? I need her help!

Bending down over the felled alien, I jam my weapon into a location I can only presume houses a heart. When there is still no movement, I cautiously start to pry the horned helmet off the creature's head. It doesn't budge at first and I wonder if it's held down by clips or some kind of magnetism. I keep pulling and eventually it gives way a little.

Let's get a look at you.

Careful to make sure my gun hand is still ready and alert, I lift the helmet halfway off the fallen creature. A weird smell begins to waft out from beneath the protective cover.

Like burnt electronics.

Looking inside, I find a tangle of wires covering its mouth, or mandibles, or whatever the hell this thing has in place of a jaw. Tilting my head to get a better look beneath the helmet, I don't notice what's going on in the spaceship above.

What the…

Something huge slams into the side of my head and I drop into the muck. My face hits the floor with such force it leaves me dazed for at least a second; maybe two. I roll to the side and blink dirty water from my eyes. It seems someone – or something – else has dropped from the ship's belly.

There are two of them!

Before I can say a word, a giant boot fills my vision and leaves me seeing stars.

Still dazed from the unexpected blow, I'm vaguely aware of being flung away from the Paracas ship and sliding halfway up the soggy hillside. Raindrops strike my face, helping to clear the cobwebs, and slowly my vision returns. It's then that I get my first good look at the thing that ambushed me. A second, equally large alien comes into focus, this one devoid of the heavy armoured plating worn by the first.

Anne said there was only one life sign on that ship! Where did this other guy come from!?

It dawns on me then that this new arrival could almost pass for a human if not for its massive size and unusually long forehead. The creature has blood red eyes set deep within a bald head and bright orange skin that makes it look like it's been slathered with fake tan. The behemoth also wears a pair of shiny black boots and gloves over a coal-grey flight suit that is stretched so tightly over its muscular frame I fear the outfit might split if it flexes too hard.

This thing's biceps are as big as my head!

I also notice a blinking apparatus attached to its chest with two corrugated tubes sprouting from each side. The tubes dangle loosely over its belly and I find myself wondering what they're supposed to be plugged into.

A helmet maybe? Or the ship itself?

But outside all that weird, geeky stuff, it's got four limbs and a face just like the rest of us. I watch as the large humanoid kneels beside its fallen comrade, checking on its condition. The way it begins shaking its head from side to side, however, leads me to believe the prognosis is not good.

Crap! Did I accidentally kill its partner!?

"Ya little runt!" the second alien growls viciously, turning its angry gaze towards me. When it speaks, I notice its teeth are yellow and crooked. They all end in jagged points that I imagine it uses to tear into flesh.

I doubt this thing knows what a toothbrush is.

"D'ya have any idea how much it's gonna cost to replace dis 'bot and those tractor emitters!?" it continues, the UTG not required to overachieve in order to get across the menace the words carry.

"That's a robot!?" I blurt out, relieved to hear I haven't actually killed somebody.

"Of course it's a robot!" comes the response. "D'ya think I would set foot on this grimy mudball if I didn't 'ave to!?"

The furious creature begins stomping in my direction, berating me with every step.

"Who's gonna pay for all this, huh!?" the Paracas yells angrily. "I'll be lucky if the finder's fee for this world covers what I owe my Overlord! If I can't pay him back, I may as well walk myself out an airlock!"

As the bald seven-foot-tall behemoth draws closer, I frantically search the grass for my weapon.

"Lookin' for this!?" the alien taunts, picking up my pistol and holding it tantalisingly out of reach.

The Paracas tosses the weapon aside and then boots me in the stomach so hard it sends me sliding through the mud halfway up the hill. I hear my bones crack under the impact.

"Where'd ya even get a Peacekeeper on a no-tech backwater planet like dis one!?..." the Paracas starts.

Peacekeeper? Is it talking about my pistol?

"..and that translator!" the inquisition continues. "That's Olympian Alliance tech!"

Suddenly his eyes narrow and he takes another menacing step towards me, pointing an accusatory finger in my direction. "You one of those no-good space cops!?"

What is he talking about!?

"Did you crash yer Trident here!?" the Paracas continues before I can find my voice. "Was that the weird energy signature I picked up comin' from this system! Well, was it!?"

Energy signature? Could it have been the Preserver ship!? Or Anne's detonation!?

The Paracas pauses for a moment and I brace myself for another angry kick.

"How 'bout we make a deal!? You wrecked my tractor emitters 'cos you wanted to save that furry red biped, right? Start talkin' and instead of killing you, I'll take you back instead a' him," he offers, patting a silver collar strapped to his thigh.

Is that one of those terrible shock collars Eve told me about!?

"Come on, hero," the Paracas goads. "What d'ya say?"

Even if I wanted to accept the beast's offer it wouldn't be possible. My voice is gone. Staring into his vivid red eyes, I try to choke out a response; anything to delay the inevitable a moment longer. But the foot he slammed into my stomach moments ago drove all the air from my body and all that comes out are a few laboured gasps. Then, when it finally seems like I might manage a sound, it's not words that come out, but vegetable stew and goat meat. It heaves out all over the grass.

The Paracas looks at the half-digested meal with contempt. It spits on the ground then shrugs.

"Fine! You don't wanna talk tough guy!?" he roars, picking me up by the scruff of my neck like I'm little more than a puppy. "Truth is I was gonna kill ya whether you told me what I wanted to know or not!"

The Paracas flings me through the air with extraordinary ease and I land at the very top of the hill in a groaning heap.

Anne! Where are you!?

What little energy I have left is expelled in the effort required to raise my eyes from the grass. If nothing else, I'm determined to stare death in the eye as it comes trudging up the hill. Looming over me once more, I watch a slow malicious grin spread across the creature's cruel face. Raising one of its huge boots high above my head, it can't help but make one final taunt: "Time to die, runt!"

The Paracas brings its boot down hard, clearly intending to crush my skull. But somehow, I manage to summon enough strength to roll out of harm's way at the last second. The impact of his heavy foot thunders into the ground and then goes straight through the turf like a nail through wood.

I see confusion cross the Paracas' face as he loses his balance. When its other knee lands moments later, it too goes straight through the ground, accompanied by an unnatural sucking sound.

Almost instantly the creature falls in as far as its waist before becoming wedged in the newly formed hole.

What happened?

The Paracas must have stomped down on a weak point in Brien's otherwise immaculately constructed home. Far below I imagine the alien's feet hanging over the very table I was sitting at only moments earlier, nose tickled by the smell of a vegetable stew.

I hope Brien's not in there; the whole thing might come down on him.

The Paracas may be stuck, but it's not about to give up the fight.

"What the!?..." it barks, clawing for anything to help free it from its predicament and latching onto my leg.

"When I get outta this I'm gonna pull out your heart and eat it!" threatens the enraged invader through gritted teeth as I kick at the fingers that are now clasped tightly around my ankle.

Why does everything wanna eat me?

As the Paracas' thick muscular arm drags me towards my gruesome end, I search desperately for anything I can use as a weapon. I feel a surge of elation when my hand finds a fist-sized rock.

Scooping it up and clenching it in my hand, I stop resisting his pull, allowing him to draw me in nice and close. Then, to its surprise, I yell, "eat this you overgrown Oompa Loompa!"

Then I slam the stone into the alien's head as hard as I can: once, twice and three times before I feel its grip loosen. The Paracas finally stops moving with an exaggerated sigh.

Exhausted, I lay there a moment watching a trickle of purple blood run down the unconscious humanoid's elongated skull.

Damn, that was close!

The Paracas is hurt, but it's not dead. But as I listen to its laboured breathing, I feel confident it won't be waking up anytime soon.

Lifting myself up on shaky legs, I take a quick inventory of my wounds. I reach to the back of my skull and feel a giant lump covered by a gooey substance that can only be blood. Judging by the pain I feel with each breath, I've got a couple of broken ribs, too. And just a tentative touch of the region confirms my diagnosis. In fact, everywhere I look there is a bruise or contusion, so I quickly give up trying to assess them all.

That was way too close.

A weird stinging sensation on my wrist adds a strange burn mark to the mix. I honestly can't remember acquiring that one.

Did I take a hit from the plasma rifle without realising it?

Examining the wound more closely, I notice the burn forms a perfect circle all the way around my wrist. Almost like a...

Bracelet! Where's Eve's bracelet!?

Clutching my side, I limp back down the hill trying to retrace my footsteps, although there is nothing on the ground to confirm my presence but huge gouges in the turf where my body landed after each impact. Given how chopped up the landscape is, I begin to lose hope of ever finding Eve's precious gift.

I discover my Peacekeeper laying near the damaged robot and I tuck the pistol back into my waistband before continuing to search for the precious gift. Eventually, I find what I seek behind one of the landing struts, though I am at a loss to explain its condition.

What's wrong with it?

Laying in the mud, the bracelet glows and writhes as if suddenly alive! Its serpent-like motions bring to mind memories of...

The Hunger!

"Adam?" Anne says, startling me half to death.

"Anne!?" I whirl on her, the quick movement combined with my head injury cause a wave of nausea to hit my stomach. It's enough to make me stumble and I grab onto the nearby landing strut to keep from falling.

"Where the hell have you been?" I manage. "I was almost killed!"

"I was staying out of the way, of course. As you will recall, I suggested you should do the same thing," she replies unapologetically.

I've never hated that impassive, apathetic voice more than I do right now.

"Why!?" I splutter, a question fuelled by frustration and pain. "What the hell is going on around here!?"

Looking at the spaceship, the Paracas, my ribs, I'm unsure where to start my line of questioning. Eventually I look down at the object behaving so unnaturally on the ground and decide to start there. "Why the hell is my bracelet acting like that!?"

Anne, of course, appears to share none of my confusion. "It is suffering from chronoton burn."

When confusion remains etched across my face, she adds: "Or to put it more simply, it has fallen victim to a time paradox. Your intervention here has sent ripples through time. The bracelet is currently being erased from existence."

Suddenly there's a sinking feeling in the pit of my stomach as a new fear stabs at me. "But if the bracelet is being erased does that mean..."

"Yes, its creator is also being erased," Anne replies with unnerving calmness.

Eve! What have I done!?

Chapter 13
???

I remember this feeling. It's familiar. A pressure building up inside my head just as I cross into the light that feels so… so… uncanny. It's a portal. Yes, I remember now. When I entered this portal, I did so with two other companions. I remember that one of them was a man. An injured man, whom I have very strong feelings for called...

Oh, and that the other was a woman, like me. Well, not exactly like me. This other woman was something more than what she appeared to be.

What was the man's name!? Alan!? No, that doesn't sound right!

I remember that we were being chased by something big. And dangerous. I remember thinking as we crossed into the bright light of the portal that if we could just make it across the threshold, we'd find a place of safety. But if I can remember all this, why can't I remember me name? Who I am? Or how I wound up in this place?

None of this seems right!

Those people who were with me are not here now. I'm alone. Alone in this endless void. There is no up or down. No left or right. Just a white luminous nothingness in every direction. It's so thick and all-consuming that I feel like I'm drowning in it. Like I'm disappearing into it and becoming nothing.

Erased.

As pieces of me continue slipping away, I struggle to hang onto one particular memory. The memory of the man. The one who came for me when I was alone and scared. He always finds me when I'm in trouble. What is his name? It's right on the tip of my tongue.

Adam! His name's Adam! And he will come for me! He always comes for me!

But even as I attempt to reassure myself, I realise I can no longer picture his face. And I'm certain soon his name will be lost to me once again. And I know that if I forget his name, he will never be able to find me. I will be lost forever. Not even a memory. And trapped here in this space; this space between. I try to scream, but my voice is gone. My brain is crumbling. Drifting. Who am I? I form one last thought and blast it out into the white.

Hurry, Adam! I'm not sure how much longer I can hang on!

Then terror – true terror – takes hold. The last memory I recall having before losing all sense of self, is of a small grey creature with a bulbous head and large black eyes. I see it engulfed by some kind of translucent monster and remember watching as this living fluid ravenously devoured the alien being. Dissolving the skinny creature until there is nothing left to prove its existence. And now I know exactly how that poor soul felt.

In the end all Scales must be balanced.

Chapter 14
ADAM X

Standing in the pouring rain, surrounded by the aftermath of my encounter with the Paracas, I try desperately to make sense of Anne's words. She said Eve is being erased from existence because of something I did. But what? I don't want to believe it even as I stare down at the proof.

What else could explain her bracelet lying in the wet grass, burning as it dissolves into nothingness. As if it's just being consumed by The Hunger. Water droplets hiss and turn to steam as they strike its white-hot surface.

Is it really undergoing what Anne suggests? Is this what chronoton burn looks like? Shifting from existence into a state where it was never created in the first place? What else could cause such a violent reaction in an otherwise ordinary piece of jewellery?

Oh my god! It's true! Why did Anne bring me here!? This is all her fault!

"What the hell have you done!?" I scream at her. "You said you brought me here to stop a time paradox, not create one!"

"You appear to be mistaken, Adam. It was not I who interrupted this nexus point. It was you," she replies, her voice as straight as steel; her mask a taciturn wall I feel a near uncontrollable urge to punch.

"What the hell are you talking about!?" I yell in disbelief. "What did I do wrong?!"

"You have just interfered with the origins of the Floran people," Anne relays, pausing briefly to give my inferior brain time to process this mind-blowing information.

The Florans?

"You see Brien was destined to be the first Human abducted and enslaved by the Paracas scout," Anne continues. "Right now, he is supposed to be lying prone on that ship, his blood freezing in preparation for the voyage back to the Paracas overlords for consideration. But he is not. He is running through the rain naked."

I gaze into the rain trying to get my head around what Anne is implying. "Are you saying that in choosing to save Brien I've just lost Eve," I manage around the hard lump forming in my throat.

Anne ignores the question. "There is more. Your act of preventing this scout from departing with Eve's earliest ancestor means that the existence of Earth remains a mystery to his masters. Your act has therefore nullified multiple future abductions from this world, and all those who would have been born as a result."

Brien was Eve's ancestor!? How many people did I just wipe out by saving him!?

Anne's head tilts slightly to the right. It's as if her circuits are crunching so many numbers, she can no longer keep her head upright.

Anne could probably tell me the exact number, but do I dare ask!?

As I ponder this, Anne's head snaps back up and she gives me an odd look of contemplation. Then, as if in answer to my unasked question, she says: "I will need more information before I can process the full ramifications of your actions. I cannot be sure what impact this change will have on the production of Elixir over time, or to those who would have become addicted and how that would have impacted their lives. I have come up with over one trillion permutations so far, and that's before I look into the impact on Earth incurred by having many of its humans remain on the planet longer than destiny had intended. Would you like to hear what I have so far?"

She's kidding, right?

"There must be a way to undo it!" I plead, ignoring her doomsday forecast. "I need to save her… we must… her… um, the girl."

What's going on?

"The girl with the pointy ears," I finally burst out in exasperation. "Freakin' Evelyn? Erin? Eve! Eve god dammit. We need to save Eve. Why can't I say her… whose bracelet…"

Anne finally jumps to my rescue. "Yes, Eve. When she moves into a state outside of existence the matter from which she was made and the matter she disturbed during her life, including that which forms your memories, will return to their original states."

Oh no!

"I will forget her?" I manage to ask, the full impact of the situation widening my eyes the length of my face.

"That would be an inaccurate statement," Anne continues. "You would have never met her in order to forget her. She'd just cease."

Eve. Eve. Eve. Say it and say it and don't forget, Adam.

But what if I do forget. Or just live in a place where I never knew her at all. In a moment from now I'll just be standing on a grassy hill in the rain as the guy who saved Brien and kicked some Paracas' butt. Erin…

Eve!

Eve won't be hurt, because she never existed. I won't be hurt as I'd never know I'd lost her. For all I know this has happened to me before and I'm none the wiser. How would I know? What if Eve was to become little more than déjà vu?

No way!

Other thoughts creep in then. Thoughts that bring tears to my eyes. I think about the red curls of her hair tucked behind those pointy little ears. Of the taste of her lips. The look in her eyes when I held out my hand and she grabbed it, hoping beyond hope, that I could be the one to save her. She deserves to exist; she's earned it. And this place, this universe, it needs her.

I need her.

"I must save her Anne," comes my voice, quiet as a mouse as if deadened by a sadness so heavy it could unbalance a galaxy.

Anne pauses ever so slightly. "The fact that the bracelet still exists means the changes to the timeline are not yet set. As long as the bracelet remains in a state of chronoton burn, there is still a chance to correct this course of action. I fear, however, that you will not like what needs to be done in order to do so."

I find myself rubbing at the X on my forehead, a move Anne eyes curiously. My fingers stop their irritation as the solution suddenly dawns on me and my stomach begins tying itself in knots. The pain in my gut doubles when Anne adds: "I cannot help you. You must correct this mistake on your own."

"I understand," I reply with a gasp, my body now numb from shock. "Whatever it takes, I'll fix this."

Willing myself into action, I prepare for the unpleasant task ahead. Returning to Brien's little hideaway, I peer through the entryway and find him in a frenzy. His eyes dart nervously as he scans his home.

At least Brien remembered to put his pants back on.

Rushing about, he picks up an assortment of items and chucks them into his canoe, which now sits open-side-up just inside the entrance.

Clearly, his plan is to return to the mainland or seek out some other island to call home. And after what he's just been through, I can't say I really blame him.

The boat may be well made, but it's quite small and if he continues to throw his life's possessions in there, it won't be long before it will struggle to hold his stodgy frame as well.

Standing silently in the entrance, I watch him continue filling the seafaring vessel with mementos and tools. A sudden thunderclap from above causes the pigs to start squealing wildly and Brien halts his mad packing to look upwards.

As he does a droplet of purple blood lands right on his cheek and I follow his gaze up to the limp alien legs dangling through the ceiling. The Paracas is wedged in their tight. Tight enough to keep the rain out, yet somehow a trickle of blood has found its way down into Brien's once peaceful home.

Maybe I hurt that Paracas bastard worse than I first thought?

Suddenly his eyes dart towards the door and he spots me. Fear and shock momentarily vanish from his kind features, overtaken by visible relief. His gratitude is made all the clearer when he rushes over and pulls me into a big bear hug.

Lost in my own thoughts, I barely register the shooting pain his embrace brings to my broken ribs.

Grinning, Brien drags me inside, then moves beneath the dangling alien and reaches up to give one of its enormous boots an experimental poke. My return has clearly given him the impression that the threat has been dealt with. Little does he know the danger is far from over.

Fumbling for the right words, all I manage to murmur is; "I'm sorry," knowing full well he won't understand me as my translator is still set to Paracas. As the device regurgitates my words in the attacking alien's native tongue, Brien's brow furrows in confusion.

Does he sense what I'm about to do?

Before he has time to react, I pull out my pistol and fire a stun blast point-blank between his shoulder blades. His eyes fix on mine hoping to find some sort of reason for the surprise attack. Then he begins a slow fall forward. I catch the poor man's body as he keels over and guide him gently to the ground, refusing to look away as his eyes glaze over.

Could he see the regret in my eyes? The shame? The guilt?

Choking back my self-hatred, I let a shiver wash down my spine. The terrible deed is done and with my thumb I gently wipe the spot of purple blood from the poor man's face. Then I get to work.

Dangling above my head, I can see the Paracas shock collar is still strapped to the alien's thigh. I knock it down with the canoe paddle and then struggle to get the contraption underneath Brien's thick red beard. With a little fiddling, I manage to get the device locked securely around his throat.

This is an atrocity. I will never forgive myself for this.

All I can do is sigh, however, as I begin dragging Brien's unconscious body towards the door. As I pull him out onto the slippery grass and mud, an odd thought enters my mind. Compelled to obey it, I release his legs and walk back into Brien's home.

A squeal greets me from the pigpen as I walk over. I release the poor creatures from captivity and they immediately set themselves to sniffing out the plentiful amounts of food stashed about Brien's home. Satisfied, I return to the grisly task at hand.

Delivering this poor soul and countless others into a lifetime of slavery. Condemning millions more to become addicts to the drug those slaves will be forced to create. Giving birth to the Floran race and...

And saving Eve.

XXXX

Anne is nowhere to be seen. I'm sure she must be watching from somewhere, but when she said she had to stay out of this nexus point, she clearly meant it. Bordering on complete exhaustion, I somehow manage to drag Brien's body back over the hill so I can lay it beneath the Paracas Scout Ship.

I'm basically gift-wrapping him.

Shaking off my reservations, I remove the man's vest and take it back up the hill to his would-be captor. I use it to bandage the unconscious alien's head wound. As a small act of defiance, I don't dig the monster out, however, leaving it to dig itself free once it awakens.

Task complete I step back down the hill, only for dizziness to start wrapping its fingers around my brain. The shock, I realise, is beginning to wear off and before I even have a chance to get a hand to my mouth, I realise I'm vomiting. What little is left in my stomach heaving out onto the mud.

What have I done!?

"Congratulations, Adam," comes a familiar voice.

I look up, not even bothering to wipe away the tendrils of spew and snot I know are still dangling from my face as I seek out her face. Anne emerges from the dark behind the Paracas ship, my polar opposite in appearance. Serene, calm and collected, the rain seemingly parting around her as if she's not even really there.

"You have repaired the timeline and saved Eve," comes that irritating voice.

She hands me the bracelet and when I fail to reach out and grab it, she drops it into the palm of my hand. It now appears completely restored. In fact, even the burns that moments earlier circled my wrist have vanished. It's like it never happened. I cast my eyes towards Brien's motionless body.

But at what cost?

Unable to hold it in any longer, I let out a howl of anguish, followed by an array of deep sobs. Anne looks on curiously, making it clear the rain isn't hiding the tears streaming from my eyes.

"What was the point of all this?" I scream at her, clutching the piece of jewellery close to my chest.

"To show you that you do not belong here. You do not belong in this time," she explains, gesturing at our ancient surroundings. "To make you understand the danger your presence in this era poses."

When I don't immediately answer, she adds: "You cannot have a life here, Adam."

Unconvinced I urge her to continue: "What are you trying to say, Anne?"

"I am suggesting you consider returning to your home in the twenty-first century," she reveals.

The twenty-first century!

"Are you kidding me!" I laugh without a hint of mirth. "That's the point you were trying to make!? That I should go home!? You could have just said that from the start! I'd be more than happy to leave this time period! Let's go get Eve and get the hell out of here!"

"No, Adam. You do not understand. I am suggesting you should return to the twenty-first century. Not Eve," Anne pauses ever so briefly. "She still has an important role to fulfil here. She cannot be allowed to go with you."

"What are you talking about? What role?" I query. "Her presence here should be even worse than mine. At least I'm from this planet, originally. As in originally originally; before I was cloned. Surely she is just as capable of mucking things up as I am."

In fact, given some of her recent decisions, perhaps even more so.

"I cannot tell you precisely why she is important to the future of your planet," Anne responds cryptically." But I can assure you she will live a long, happy life and be revered by many."

This isn't making any sense at all.

I stare long and hard at Anne trying to find reason. There's something not right about all of this. Maybe it's the mask, but I get a sense Anne isn't telling me the truth. But why would she lie now? She hasn't lied to me before.

But she sure has omitted key facts!

I'm relieved to hear Eve has a future, at the very least. But a future without me? After what I've just gone through; after what I've just done to save her. I can't just walk away from her.

"But I… we… we're supposed to…" I stumble, but the words drift off meaninglessly into the wind.

You almost killed her today Adam; you almost wiped her from existence.

My heart sinks and my face contorts with the realisation that Anne might be right. If Eve can no longer be a part of my future, how does she find out about it? Does she just find herself alone and afraid and wounded in the desert?

Will she ever know where I went? Or why?

"What about you?" comes the question without any bidding. "Will you come with me?"

"No, I will need to remain behind as well," she tells me. "Someone will need to protect Eve in your stead."

"So you expect me to give up everything!" I blurt aghast. "Now! After you've come back from the dead! After Eve and I have finally found ourselves and our place in this world?"

Should I do it then? Should I just go home and forget about the both of them?

I'd given up on returning to civilisation and a world of modern conveniences. Yet now it's being handed to me on a silver platter. Microwaves, pizza, television; toilet paper! All it will cost me is the two people I care about most in the world.

No, I won't do it! The price is too high!

There must be another way. I refuse to accept this. My brain begins tripping over itself as I search for some way out. Some alternative solution. Then it clicks.

Anne suggested I leave, but when does she ever suggest anything?

"Wait a second! You only said 'suggest,'" I point out, clutching at straws. "You didn't say I had to go. You only suggested it. That means there's some grey area, right? Some other plan."

"You are correct," she confirms, and I can immediately feel the reluctance weighing down her answer. "Technically you do not have to leave, but staying will mean facing more morally ambiguous situations like the one you faced today. What will happen the next time you have to do something distasteful in order to prevent a time paradox?"

"Like I said before, I'll do it. I'll do whatever must be done," I insist, stubbornly.

"What if the next paradox requires you to kill somebody?" she parries.

"If I have to, I have to," I respond, sounding more certain than I actually feel.

Anne takes off her mask so she can look me in the eyes, and the impact of seeing her soft face sucks the air from my lungs.

"I do not believe you, Adam," she starts gently. "You are a good man with a strong sense of what is right and wrong. It took everything you had just to deliver Brien into a life of slavery. If I had told you that you had to kill him in order to prevent this paradox, I do not believe you could have done so."

"You're wrong! To save the woman I love I would do absolutely anything!" I yell back, the outburst surprising even myself.

*Oh my God! I just admitted to loving Eve...
and the first person I told was Anne!*

Anne is unmoved by my passionate plea. "That is all the more reason to leave. You almost erased the woman you love because of some misguided sense of morality and look what you had to do to get her back. Look at Brien. How many times will you be able to correct these paradoxes before you begin hating yourself? Before you become everything you despise? How do you think it will impact Eve to see you suffer like that?"

Why is she saying these horrible things? She doesn't even sound like Anne anymore.

"Me!? This is all on you, lady!" I throw the blame back at her, pointing an accusing finger at her face. "You're the one that brought me to this stupid island and almost made me wipe Eve from existence! She was safe until you insisted I go with you!"

"Safe? Did you believe she was safe before this incident?" Anne asks rhetorically. "Allow me to enlighten you, Adam. Eve ran away because she was dying of radiation poisoning and she was too afraid to tell you."

What?!

This revelation cuts deep and I find myself at a loss for words. I think back to her head burrowed beneath the camel skins, refusing to show me anything more than her pale cheeks. The sweat on her brow and fear in her eyes. And I know it's true. Somehow, I think I always knew.

The portals! I'd managed to convince myself that even without nanites, her limited exposure had kept her safe!

Anne pushes forward into the sudden quiet. "What do you suppose would have happened if I had not intervened and cured her of this affliction?"

How could I have been so stupid!?

"Knowing this, do you still maintain that you are the best person to protect her?" she finishes.

The wind knocked out of me, I swing from my knees to my butt, not even caring if it lands in my spew. I sit there for a full minute before answering. My mind swirling in time with the rain and wind, seeking some path out of the growing tornado. A path where Eve and I can remain together and stay safe. In the end, the only thing I can think to say is: "You're right, Anne. I was a fool to think I could protect her."

"I am sorry, Adam," she apologises. "I did not want to hurt you like this. I had hoped that once you understood that an unwavering desire to do good is not always enough, you would choose to leave without a need for me to reveal Eve's illness."

"I get it; I do," I sigh. "And I guess I don't blame you. This is my fault. Classic Adam! Being stubborn right up until the last moment. I always think I know what's best for everybody. What was that thing you always used to say to me about good and evil?"

"That they are subjective," she reminds me.

"Yeah, that. I never really got what that meant until now. I guess you were right all along, huh? About my desire to do good not always being enough." I shake my head, weary and deflated. "So long as I stay here I'm always going to try to do what I think is right regardless of the effect it might have on the timeline, aren't I? And that's why I need to go. It's too dangerous doing things my way."

"I am glad you see that now, Adam," Anne offers my slumped shoulders. "I know this is not easy for you."

"But you've gotta let me see her one more time." I plead. "After everything that's happened, I need to know she's okay. I need her to know I didn't run out on her. Can you do this for me?"

Please do this for me.

Anne slips her mask back over her face. "Of course," she states, waving a portal into existence. "I expected as much."

I step over Brien's body and into the light, towards the darkness beyond.

Chapter 15
EVE

As suddenly as it all began, it ends. The nightmare of all nightmares. The dread of being systematically erased from existence pulses out from my body with one heaving breath. Then when I inhale, my memories return like a tsunami rushing in from the sea. It brings with it an awareness that, while I do once again exist in this universe, I am not yet fully awake. I am still stuck in a dream world.

Eventually I recall the smell of the fire lizard's breath. And then the pain in my ankle. Of course! I'm still reliving that first meeting with Adam. Those first steps in what would become our long journey together. But what happened after that chase? Where did we end up next?

I remember as soon as I feel that searing heat at my back. I'm lying on a bed of hot sand. I can feel millions of tiny granules clinging to my exposed flesh and face. After three years of living in an arid desert, you'd think I would have become accustomed to it by now. But I hate sand; even in my dreams. It's coarse and rough and irritating...

And it gets everywhere!

Brushing the annoying grit from my lashes, I open my eyes and see a baleful red sun intensely glaring down at my body. The familiar skies that surround it are a beautiful aquamarine.

This is the Buudaki habitat.

Looking around confirms my initial suspicion: I am once again reliving my own history. It occurs to me I should be annoyed by this, but the truth is I'm just relieved to be free of that horrible white void. The memory of having my identity stripped away piece by piece causes an involuntary shiver to run the length of my spine.

I will happily take dreaming about my past over that godforsaken place any day.

Speaking of the past, I find the rest of the desert enclosure much as I remember it. Nearby rests the fire lizard's massive, decapitated head. A result of the creature's foolish attempt to follow us through the portal in pursuit of a tasty meal. Pushed up against its snout I see Adam, straining to pry open the reptile's yellow teeth, his efforts made all the more difficult now that he only has one hand.

Why is he doing that anyway!?

For one crazy moment I wonder if he's trying to retrieve his lost limb. But then I recall what happened the last time we were here. Anne was swallowed by the beast the moment we arrived, at which point Adam leapt into action desperately trying to get her out.

Not that she needed any help.

Right on cue, the animal's jaws begin to shudder, then slowly part. Not due to Adam's one-armed efforts, but because Anne is using her considerable strength to free herself from within. When the mouth is spread wide enough, she jumps clear and it slams shut behind her.

Even in my dreams, I can't be rid of her! At least she looks terrible.

The android's crystalline endoskeleton is covered in thick lizard saliva, which drips from her and sizzles on the hot sand.

And smells even worse!

Mashed amongst the saliva is fragments of Adam's arm. It's enough to flood the back of my throat with bile. I look to Adam expecting to see him mirroring my disgust, but the only expression I find on his handsome face is pure joy. Watching the way he smiles at her, with so much warmth and affection, I feel that old jealousy once again rearing its ugly head.

Enjoy this moment while you can, machine! In the real world, you're nothing but radioactive dust.

The spiteful thought has only just crossed my mind when Adam suddenly keels over. It seems the blood loss and shock from losing an arm has finally proved too much for him.

It's then that I wonder if this is somehow the work of the Great Cosmic Scales. Hurting the man I love to punish me for my hateful thoughts.

There's no escaping the Scales it seems, even in my dreams.

XXXX

Deep down I know everything that is happening here is a dream. I know I'm not really in the Buudaki habitat. I'm just unconscious on Earth. But the knowledge does little to lessen the pain I feel watching Adam die.

Thankfully, even in my nightmares, Anne refuses to let that happen. After his collapse, she takes him into the shade of the giant lizard's head and tends to his injury as best she can. I hover anxiously nearby for what seems like an age as the android works on his arm and when she finally does step away the wound is miraculously puckered and closed.

Adam has mentioned he heals faster than other humans, but can he really heal that quickly?

Anything's possible in a dream, I suppose.

Her job done, Anne disappears from view for a while, presumably to start the process of regenerating her own missing flesh. I begin a silent vigil, praying to the Scales that Adam will continue to get better.

It hurts seeing him so fragile and pale.

My hopes of getting a moment with him alone are short-lived. Adam's awakening coincides almost perfectly with Anne's return, and as predicted the android is back to her annoyingly beautiful self. Just seeing her smooth white skin, dark chestnut hair and enviable curves makes my blood boil.

That annoyingly perfect machine did save Adam's life. And not just in my dreams, either.

When I first met Adam all those years ago, I was immediately smitten with him. He was handsome and brave, and he took me in when I was at my lowest point. I remember feeling a twinge of jealousy when I first saw Anne, but it was nothing compared to the rage I feel now.

I guess it wasn't as bad before as Adam wasn't really mine. Now that we're together though, I can barely stand to look at her.

That realisation makes me ashamed of myself. When this happened for real, we were not rivals. I was just a lost girl, confused out of my brain and scared as hell.

I should better recognise Anne's actions both past and present. Yes, Adam did love her, I'm sure of that now. But now he loves me. And I should work harder to keep my snide thoughts and feelings from poisoning my heart in the here and now.

Chapter 16
ADAM X

As promised, Anne returns me to my desert camp at the exact same moment in time we had originally departed. And as usual, I'm the first one through to the other side of the portal. As my feet touch the ground, I catch the briefest glimpse of my own back entering a portal on the other side of the village ruins. The moment is unnerving at best, if not outright horrifying.

What would happen if I had actually met my past self? Would one of us combust or collapse into a black hole or something?

But before I have a chance to contemplate this possibility further something else catches my eye. It's past Anne, just moments after my past self disappears into the light. She hangs back a moment rather than following the pre-Paracas, pre-Brien, pre-time paradox Adam through the doorway and into Scotland.

What is she waiting for?

Unmasked, she turns to stare at me with those perfect sapphire eyes and asks me a single question: "What did you end up deciding?"

"I'm leaving," I answer, sullenly.

"For what it is worth, I am sorry," she apologises.

"Yeah, the other you just said the same thing and no, it's not worth much," I tell her, coldly.

With that, Anne follows my counterpart through the portal and I could swear she looks genuinely hurt as she turns away. Their doorway blinks out of existence moments later leaving me to ponder her strange reaction alone.

> *Don't fool yourself, Adam!? Anne doesn't feel a damn thing! She never has and never will!*

The masked, present day version of Anne reappears then, and in doing so, provides the perfect target for my growing hostility.

"Just had an interesting conversation with the past you," I tell her, each word dripping with resentment and spite. "So, I guess you knew I was going to leave this entire time, huh?"

"I did," she admits.

"Why couldn't you tell me what was going to happen from the start!?" I scream, no longer able to contain my rage. "Why make me jump through all these hoops when I never really had a choice to begin with!?"

"I have already explained this to you, Adam, numerous times," comes her cool response, clearly unmoved by my reaction. "You would not have believed me if I had simply explained to you what needed to happen. I knew the only way you would ever accept the truth was if you witnessed the consequences of your actions firsthand."

Consequences?! Are you serious?! I just created a race of slaves!

"If I had thought there was any other way, I assure you I would have tried it," she continues. "I knew you would attempt to rescue Brien and in so doing create a future where Eve did not exist, but I did not foresee any difficulties undoing your changes. Your stun weapon should have given you a decisive advantage in your dual against the Paracas. I apologise for both the mental and physical stress you have suffered as a result of my actions."

Maybe it would have been better if I had lost to the Paracas?

Deep down I know Anne's right and I believe she would have spared me this pain if she could. And I'd like to think she would have stepped in if I was about to lose that fight against the Paracas! To risk so much just to prove a point, though, seems to suggest things would've gotten pretty bad had I stayed oblivious to my impact on the world.

Yet even with those concessions, I can't quell the fire burning inside me. I'm furious with her for the part she played in this cruel charade.

"God damn it, Anne! I'm so mad at you right now I don't even wanna look at you!" I burst, seething.

"I understand your frustration," she says simply. "If I had just taken you away from Eve to some future time without any explanation, or without proof to back up my assertions, you would have hated me all the same. Only you would have hurt far worse and for far longer. For what it is worth, I am..."

"Yeah, yeah! You're sorry!" I interrupt before she can finish her robotic platitude. "You're starting to sound like a broken record, you know that! Why don't you just go get the first jump home ready while I go say goodbye to..."

The love of my life?

I turn away from Anne and storm towards the main hut in the centre of the village. The one in which my past self had placed an unconscious, recovering Eve only moments earlier.

It already feels like a lifetime ago.

As I stride towards a one-sided conversation that I'm truly dreading, I take one last dig at the one I blame for putting me in this predicament. "The sooner you and I part ways the better off we'll all be."

Chapter 17
EVE

This dream, this endless dream, is just so odd. On one hand, it reminds me of the Great Cosmic Scales; tipping back and forth in their eternal struggle to balance good and bad in the universe. Except in this dream state it's fact and fiction that are constantly seesawing back and forth.

At least on the fiction side of things, the one-armed Adam has returned to full health, more or less. This has enabled events to again resume a familiar course.

As before, Anne presents me with a set of handmade garments made from fire lizard leather. After I put them on, I return Adam's beloved jacket to its rightful owner and the three of us proceed to the outer ring of the Preserver ship in search of escape pods.

When we arrived here previously, a great debate ensued over whether or not it was safe to go back for Adam's friend, Zanatos. And after deciding we would wait for Anne's pulse emitter to recharge, a series of terrifying encounters soon followed. We came face-to-face with the Preserver who had abducted us, then narrowly escaped the parasitic Hunger as it began feeding on our skinny, grey captors.

This time around, however, events begin to skew as soon as we set foot into the featureless corridors of the ship's outer ring. As I emerge from the portal, Anne suddenly grabs my arms and pins them painfully behind my back.

What the Hela is she doing!?

I try to protest, but I'm quickly reminded that in this dream I am unable to speak. So, I do the only thing I can. I struggle against the android's restraining hands in a futile effort to escape her vice-like grip.

Blast her! She's too damn strong!

With his back facing me, I grunt at Adam imploring him to free me. But when he finally does turn, all I see is a sad resignation in his eyes. Reaching into his jacket he pulls out a familiar looking glove.

That's impossible!

I wore that jacket for hours! There's no way the universal translator was in that pocket! I would have noticed for sure.

Possible or not, the UTG is now present and Adam activates it with his thumb so he can speak to me. I realise it's the first time since this whole crazy nightmare began that I've been able to understand what he's been saying.

Finally, I can get some answers!

"I'm so sorry about this, Eve," my lover begins. "Really, I am. I'm finally getting to go home and I want nothing more than to take you with me. But Anne says she can't let that happen; that we can't let that happen. According to Anne, you're meant for something greater than me and even as pissed off as I am with her right now, I know deep down she's right. You're meant for something better than a boring life in the suburbs with me it seems."

No! I want to go with you, Adam! I don't care what Anne says!

I try to say as much, but still no words come out. It's as if fate's cold hands are gripped around my neck, suffocating the words before they can escape. And the more desperate I become, the harder I choke.

"You've always looked at me like I'm some kind of hero, Eve," Adam's sad voice continues. "I've tried to be that for you. But the truth is I have no idea what I'm doing here. I knew radiation was a risk when I took you with us, but I convinced myself that freeing you was more important."

You were right! I would have died a lot sooner if you hadn't taken me with you!

"I was so sure that two portals wouldn't be enough to cause you any permanent harm. And my arrogance could've gotten you killed. It was dumb luck that Anne somehow survived the explosion and turned up to cure you. I think it's time we accept that I don't know how to keep you safe and I never did. She'll do a much better job protecting you than I ever could. I just wanted to say… I just think you should know… you know… I love..."

But before he can finish, he breaks into tears. I want to reach for him, but Anne's cold hands only squeeze tighter. I continue to struggle in vain. Adam seems unaware, tears washing down his face as he looks vacantly into the featureless grey floors of the corridor.

No, this is wrong! This is all wrong!

My mind begins to race as I look for a way to stop what's unfolding. To tip the Scales back from fiction to fact. What is happening right now? Is this still a dream? How could Adam know about Anne's explosion while we're still on the alien ship? That happened after we escaped from the Preservers. How could he know about my radiation poisoning? And what does he mean about Anne surviving? Is it Anne behind Tiamat's mask? Is that it? Wait, this isn't a dream, is it? His voice sounds so real. I can feel his breath. I can hear his sobs. Is this real?

Let me out!!!

My silent scream echoes about my head until Adam steps in closer. He gently brushes his fingers over my cheek and says, "take care, Eve. I'll never forget you."

Kissing me so softly and sweetly that I feel it lingering on my lips long after he has pulled away, he enters an escape pod and launches into space, leaving me devastated and alone.

No! This is not real! None of this is real! Wake up, Eve! WAKE UP, NOW!

Then his accursed android yanks me violently back into the portal.

Chapter 18
ADAM X

Tears come like a thunderstorm, attempting to wash my anguish away. After confessing all my failings to Eve, the words I really wanted to say got caught in my throat. Instead I wipe the tears from my eyes and take a deep breath. I lean in and run a finger down Eve's soft cheek, then give her one last, long, final kiss. Her lips seem to respond to my touch, and it takes a monumental effort to pull myself away.

A gust of wind moves through the hut then, and it sounds like an anguished moan.

> *It reminds me of Eve's sobbing when I first discovered her in the Flora One habitat.*

Physically and emotionally drained, I stand up and leave the hut. I believe what I said to her: that Anne will keep her safe better than I ever could.

> *I'm sure I do.*

But that truth doesn't make the reality of the situation any easier to swallow. Or lessen the feelings of anger I have towards Anne.

Fuelling my self-loathing even further is the heavy lump of shame I feel in the pit of my stomach. A deep-seated guilt that lingers like a shadow under everything that I'm feeling and experiencing. I must admit there is a part of me that's actually relieved all this craziness is over. That I can run away from it all and return to a place of comfort. A place where I'm not Adam X, clone defender and protector of Eve. But as Adam Furst, pain-in-the-butt police officer and son to Henrietta Furst.

*At least now I never have to look Eve in the
eye and tell her she's a clone.*

I find myself rubbing at the X and the motion disturbs a small scab on my forehead that I wasn't aware was there. A thin trickle of blood runs over my brow and down my nose. Is this it then? Is this what I am?

A coward?

It must be true. Why else would I hate myself for being so glad that Anne has come along and given me the excuse I need to run away from all this. But I know part of me is already thinking of hot showers and hotter food. And of my flatscreen TV. Such thoughts surely confirm my cowardice.

*And a coward like me doesn't deserve the
love of a good woman like Eve.*

"The first portal is prepared, Adam. Are you ready?" Anne asks, as I lift my face to the blazing sun and instinctively strip off my jacket.

I realise then that all my clothes, which were completely soaked upon our return from Scotland, are now bone dry. The water evaporating along with the hopes and dreams I had for Eve and me.

"Wait! I forgot something," I stall, rushing back inside the hut with my coat in hand.

Knowing how much Eve has always loved my leather jacket, I make a last-minute decision to leave it for her. I place it lovingly at the foot of her bed, then remove the Universal Translation Glove and lay it on top. I'm going to miss them both.

I won't be needing it where I'm going.

I briefly consider leaving her the pistol as well, before remembering Eve hates using it. She'll always opt for her bow and arrows. And anyway, Anne is basically a walking weapon with power beyond the scale of anything this would will see for thousands of years.

Besides, all the gifts in the world won't make you feel less guilty about leaving her, Adam.

"Okay, now I'm ready," I tell Anne, as I emerge from the hut for the second time. "Oh, and I'm sorry about the way I spoke to you before. It means a lot to me knowing you'll be here to take care of Eve."

"There is no need to apologise, Adam. This is a difficult situation for all involved," she replies. "But you can rest assured I will protect her with the same dedication I did your previous iterations."

With that in mind, I take a good long look around and try hard to memorise all the small details, pausing every so often to examine things more closely as I make my way towards the already opened portal.

I can't believe this is the last time I'm ever gonna see this place.

Looking at the drafty old huts, the soot-covered fire pit and the scattered ceramic pots left behind by the previous inhabitants, I realise at some point in the past year this primitive little camp really has become home. I'm actually going to miss it.

Joni Mitchell was right: you don't know what you've got 'till it's gone.

Even with a mask and robe covering Anne from head to toe, there seems to be a note of impatience in the way she carries herself. With her superior intelligence, I have no doubt she noticed I've been stalling, but she is also smart enough not to comment on the fact and I find myself grateful for this small courtesy.

Then I see the arrow bone, just where Eve had left it. Pointing deep into the Earth rather than the direction she had run from me. Prepared to die alone in the wild rather than make me face a reality in which I was helpless to truly save her.

Okay, Adam. Enough screwing around. It's time to go.

I finally begin walking steadily towards the doorway of light with all the enthusiasm of a man being led to the electric chair.

With Anne falling into step behind me, I continue moving forward, absently noting she has opened this latest portal in the exact same spot as the previous one. The positioning of the doorways match so precisely, I can see the footprints of my past self, leading into the light. It occurs to me it's almost like they were put there to guide me towards my fate.

Hold on a second! That doesn't make any sense! Unless...

An epiphany surges through me like a bolt of lightning from the heavens. Its power sparked into existence by the soft impressions made by my previous footsteps. Like the final piece of a puzzle falling into place, everything suddenly becomes crystal clear and I know what must be done.

Spinning quickly before Anne has time to register the certainty I now possess, I draw my weapon and fire it point blank into her stomach.

It catches Anne squarely in her guts.

I'd be lying if I said I had it all figured out when I decided to pull the trigger. But I knew one thing for certain: Anne did not survive the blast that destroyed The Hunger. That wasn't her behind me, staring vacantly at my back as if lost in thought. The devil was in the details. And the evidence was as plain as day, I just couldn't see it until now.

Right there in front of the portal that heads to who-knows-where are my footprints in the sand. Just my footsteps. The steps I made on my original journey to Papa Westray.

So where are her footprints?

There are none because the dead don't walk. But beyond that one revelation, I have no idea as to the true identity of the imposter or what motivation they could have for trying to deceive me. Whatever the reason, I have to act quickly.

Thankfully, the imposter never saw it coming.

Time seems to slow as I watch the masked stranger topple backwards. The Peacekeeper lights up in my hand, still crackling from the stun blast I'd just unleashed. Before they've even hit the ground, the black robes and intricate mask fade away to reveal the truth hiding beneath. It's a sight I would recognise in an instant, anywhere and any era.

A Preserver!

Of course.

"I KNEW IT!" I yell, as the frail grey creature spasms around in the dirt.

I should've known Anne coming back from the dead was too good to be true!

I keep the gun trained on the monster, unsure how long the stun blast will last on such a powerful being.

Maybe I should just kill it now?

It's a tempting thought and I even reach for the lethal power pack still in my pocket intending to swap it out for the stun pack my pistol has currently stocked, before deciding against it. I need answers first. Why put me through all this? Why save Eve? Is that really Eve in there or is she an imposter, too? Why put on this elaborate show to separate us?

I shoot another bolt into the Preserver just to be sure it can't move and step in close. It's only then that I realise the alien is laughing, even while electricity racks its body with pain. A high, maniacal cackle that resonates deep within my skull.

"You think this is funny!?" I ask, my brows knitting together in confusion.

"No, not at all," the alien manages to reply with surprising clarity considering its body is now wracked by violent spasms. The Preserver even sounds oddly merry as it adds, "this is actually quite disastrous."

What's wrong with this thing!? Is it insane!?

"Regardless, a part of me is still incredibly relieved you did not step through that portal," the alien continues, further adding to my confusion. "How did you uncover the truth that I was not, in fact, Android Zero?"

Android Zero? I've never heard Anne called by that name before.

"Uh, the footprints. I caught a glimpse of our past selves disappearing through a doorway in the exact same spot," I answer, poking a thumb towards the sputtering portal that seems to pulsate in time with the alien's spasms. "But when I looked at the tracks we left in the dirt I noticed there was only one set. Mine. I'm guessing your past self didn't leave any footsteps 'cos you things float, right?"

"A brilliant deduction, Adam!" it praises. "Judging by what I have seen here today, I have no doubt Adam Furst would have made a fine detective one day. Had his life not been cut tragically short, of course."

This Preserver is way too happy! It's actually freaking me out!

"Cut short by you and your lot," I fire back, before curiosity gets the better of me. "Can I just say you seem to be pretty cheery for someone who just had their entire evil scheme backfire. What was the grand plan anyway? To trap me back in the Earth habitat on your ship?"

"Oh no, nothing like that I can assure you!" the words spill into my mind and somehow they sound genuine.

"I no longer have any affiliation with my people. They exiled me quite some time ago."

Actually, I think I do remember hearing something about an exiled Preserver back on their ship.

"And what I told you about Evie being sick was entirely true," it insists, vehemently. "I cured her in order to prevent a time paradox just as I said, and I truly was trying to return you to the twenty-first century as promised."

It's lying. It has to be. Why did he call her Evie?

I'm not falling for this guy's garbage. "I call BS. Why lie about who you are!? Why the big charade!? You could've come straight to Eve and I and explained everything!? Do you really think I would've stopped you from saving her life!? Can't you see how messed up pretending to be my dead friend was!? How can I possibly trust you now!?"

"I am truly sorry," it says, sounding truly sincere yet again. "I convinced myself when this all began that I had no choice but to trick you. That if I had tried to tell you the whole truth you would not be able to handle it and would have gotten too emotional to do what needed to be done. I now suspect I may have been lying even to myself. I believe the real reason I proceeded the way I did was to hurt you. I think a part of me blamed you for releasing The Hunger and getting two of my people killed."

"That was an accident!" I protest, my part in their deaths placing me on the defensive. "We never meant to release that monster from its habitat! By the time we discovered it was hiding inside Anne it was already too late!"

"I know that now," it assures me. "Travelling with you I have had the chance to observe what kind of man you really are, and I no longer believe you would harm any living being if there was another option available."

"Don't be so sure! You're not off the hook just yet!" I threaten as I raise my gun to my eyeline, but my words lack conviction.

I've never been good at interrogating perps.

Back when Adam Furst walked a beat it was his partner, Frank Morningstar, who did all the talking. He had a way of talking someone in circles until they spilled their guts.

I could really use his help right now.

"I meant no offence," the alien says softly. "I only wished to convey my belief that you are a good and honourable man."

I'm hesitating. Why am I hesitating?

Keeping this Preserver alive would be a dangerous move. But something just isn't adding up here. Three years and then suddenly this? Eve runs away and out of nowhere an enemy turns up to bring her back.

"Um, thanks I guess," I say, finally lowering my weapon a little. "Look, I can't pretend I'm not pissed about what you did to me, but you did save Eve's life, so I'm prepared to hear you out if you're willing to tell me the whole truth this time."

"I appreciate that, Adam," the alien claims. "I truly do. I should probably warn you my tale is a long one."

"Well, you said it's gonna take Eve two days to wake up, right? So, I guess I've got nothing but time on my hands. Go ahead," I urge, giving the alien permission to proceed.

"Excellent!" comes the excited response. "Allow me to start by introducing myself properly. Back on the Enclosed Dimensional Nexus, I was called Eldest, but these days I am known as Exile."

"An enclosed dimensional what now?" I interrupt, getting the feeling I'm going to need a lot of things explained to me before this is over.

"An Enclosed Dimensional Nexus, which is more often called the EDN, is the technical term for the vessel you and your friends escaped..."

But the sentence is cut short as a deluge of red suddenly splatters across Exile's face. Surprised by this unexpected event, I follow its shocked gaze down to my torso. Well, that's odd.

How did that get there?

It takes me a puzzled moment to really understand the sight. Something long and sharp has erupted through my stomach, splattering the still spasming Preserver with blood.

As the weapon is pulled free, I instinctively clutch at my side trying to stem the flow. But with a wound in both my back and front, there is no way to slow the bleeding. Soon my hand is slick and wet from the wasted effort of trying.

I can't believe it! I've been stabbed!

Spinning to confront my attacker I find nothing but the shape of a sword floating in the air. Only visible thanks to the blood clinging to its sides.

How is this happening!?

"ADAM, NO!" I hear Exile's anguished voice cry out in my mind.

It's only then that I remember Preservers can move things with their powerful minds. The memory of them using telekinesis to lift Anne and hold her steadfast to the ceiling as if she weighed nothing comes flooding back. Compared to something like that, picking up a sword and using it to stab me in the back would be child's play.

In fact, our whole conversation was probably a ruse to buy time for this monster to reach out with its mind and use this hidden blade. He had probably stashed somewhere nearby before we even went to Scotland!

Sonuvabitch played me!

"STOP!" Exile pleads as I pull the lethal power pack from my pocket, clip it to my gun and prepare to shoot him again. This time for real.

But I never get to pull the trigger a second time. Before I can line up the shot the hilt of the blade slams down hard against my wrist, knocking the Peacekeeper from my grasp and causing me to yell in equal parts pain and surprise.

Goddamned Preservers!!

As I chase my gun to the floor another invisible blow smashes the bridge of my nose so hard, I feel the bone break. The impact leaves me seeing stars and I can feel the fight leaving my body.

Dizzy; bleeding; broken. I roll onto my back and try to look through the blood pooling in my eyes. Out of seemingly thin air, a humanoid shape materialised into being, albeit missing one arm.

"What the hell?" I manage, the question barely more than a squeak.

The shape leans in closer and as soon as I get a good look at my assailant, I recognise the face. It's the face I knew would always be my demise. The enemy I could never escape.

It's me.

"Hello big fellow," the other Adam says in an all too familiar voice and with a playful glint in his eye, as if nothing of consequence had just happened.

He glances toward Exile and with a mischievous grin, says: "Guess we're doing this the hard way, huh?"

Does this other me even exist!? Or is this another one of Exile's mind tricks!

"Don't you worry about a thing champ, I'll look after her," my one-armed duplicate assures me taking a few cautious steps backwards.

Eve!

Then without warning, he launches himself in my direction and slams his boot right into my face. The last thing I'm aware of before the world goes completely dark is someone laughing.

And it sounds just like me.

Chapter 19
EVE

Groggy and disoriented, my blurry eyes open and for the briefest of moments I panic, unsure of where I am. As a familiar thatch ceiling comes into focus, however, I realise I'm back in my home and panic is quickly replaced by confusion.

How did I get back here?

Was it all a dream? Did I even leave in the first place? But that thought is squashed as soon as I realise there's a stiffness in my leg.

The arrow. The apple.

I don't understand. Did Adam come save me? I have to find him; it's time to tell him the truth. But trying to call out causes little more than a dry cough to escape from my parched throat.

"You're finally awake!" Adam's familiar voice announces happily.

Turning my head, I find him sitting by the bed, a broad grin splitting his face from ear to ear.

I go to tell him as much, but realise there's a more pressing need that must be taken care of first.

"Thirsty," I croak, clutching at my neck.

"Of course you are; you've been asleep for two days now. Here, drink this," Adam replies, scooping up water from a nearby jug then placing the cup into my shaking hands.

Desperate to banish the sandy dryness from my mouth, I guzzle the liquid too fast and some of it dribbles down my chin and soaks my chest.

"Whoa! Slow down there," he chuckles. "You'll make yourself sick."

"Oh, Adam!" I finally exclaim, dropping the cup and throwing my arms around him tightly. "I had the worst nightmare! I dreamt we were both back on the Preserver ship. But when we reached the escape pods you decided to leave me behind!"

"It was just a bad dream, Evie. You know I would never leave you. My arm on the other hand," he jokes, referring to the limb he lost while protecting me from the fire lizard.

What did he just call me?

"Eve'E?" I repeat, my eyebrow raised curiously. "Did you just call me, Eve'E?"

"That's your name, isn't it?" he frowns, creasing the familiar tattoo on his brow in such a way it almost looks wrong.

"Yes, that is my full name," I explain. "On Flora One only spouses or family members use each other's full names. It's just... that's the first time I've ever heard you say it, is all."

"I can stop using it if you want," he offers, stroking my shoulder tenderly. "But as far as I'm concerned you are my family now. I'm just sorry it took almost losing you for me to see that."

"I... I don't know what to say," I stammer, feeling the heat rush into my cheeks. "I feel the same way about you. Adam, I need to explain... about running away... I... it wasn't because of you. Well, that's not entirely true, but it's not what you think."

"I know," he assures me. "Your friend told me all about your radiation poisoning and how you were trying to spare me the pain of watching you die."

By the Scales! Tiamat! Of course! In all the excitement of seeing Adam again, I completely forgot about her!

"The woman in the mask?" I inquire. "The one that cured me? Where is she now?"

"Gone," he says, simply. "She brought you back to me, explained what happened, then just up and left without so much as a goodbye."

Many thoughts race through my head then. Who was she? Where did she come from? How did she speak Floran? And when did she learn of my reason for running away? Did I tell her when she was patching me up and just forget?

I suddenly recall my vivid dream and Adam's theory that Tiamat was actually Anne in disguise. If that were the case, it would actually answer a lot of my questions. She'd know all these things no one else could. But it does pose another query.

How did she survive the explosion?

"Adam," I begin, reluctantly. "You don't think Tiamat could actually be Anne, do you?"

"You're not serious, are you?" he asks.

The grave expression on my face lets him know that I am, and he adds: "I mean, I don't see how it could be? She blew up, right?"

"I know it sounds crazy, but she did say she could time travel, right?" I remind him. "What if she came from the past to help us? Or pulled herself back together after the explosion or something?"

"Anything's possible I suppose," Adam replies, scratching his beard. "Are you saying you think we should go after her?"

No!

In all honesty, that's not what I'm trying to say at all. The last thing I want is to discover I'm right, then have to compete with Anne for Adam's affections all over again. On the other hand, I do now technically owe her my life.

Twice now in fact.

"Do you think we should?" I ask, to avoid answering.

"I don't think we should go chasing down some stranger on the slim chance they could be Anne," he says, surprising me. "I'd much rather take the win and focus on our future instead."

That's what I want, too!

"As long as you're sure," I say, doing my best to seem nonplussed. "Besides, I'm sure you're right. If it really was Anne, why would she hide it?"

"My thoughts exactly," he nods eagerly in agreement. "I'm betting this Tiamat is some kinda wandering healer. Or maybe just a good Samaritan."

"Sa-mara-tin?" I repeat the unfamiliar word.

"Yeah, a good Samaritan. It's like a person who goes around doing good deeds with no thought of reward." he explains.

Maybe she really was a living embodiment of the Great Cosmic Scales.

"To tell you the truth, I'm less concerned about who she is and more worried about those men that attacked you. If you had been killed, I don't know what I would've done," Adam reveals.

"I'm so sorry, Adam. None of this would've happened if I had just told you the truth from the start instead of running away," I reply, examining my calf and finding no evidence that an arrow wound ever existed there.

I guess whatever Tiamat put inside that apple heals physical injuries as well as radiation!

"Well regardless, I swear I won't let any of those savages hurt you ever again!" he declares, clenching his fist to emphasise the point. "We've been living like paupers to avoid drawing attention to ourselves for too long! Well, no more! I think it's high time I built you a real home! No more living in squalor!"

Skwa-ler?

Rather than inquire about this second unfamiliar word, I decide to ask a more pressing question: "What do you mean 'real home?'"

"I mean, you and I are the smartest people on this whole stupid planet! We should be living like royalty, in a castle or a temple! Don't worry, I'll work out the details," he assures me, sounding more certain than I've ever heard him before. "By the time I'm done, this land will be a safe place to live and no one will dare think of harming either of us ever again. What d'ya say, Evie? You wanna build a new world with me?"

A new world?

Is that a good idea? Isn't there a chance we could accidentally change this planet's history? Adam's decision to keep us moving in those first few years always made a lot of sense to me. We had to be sure our presence here didn't inadvertently cause some sort of time paradox and the best way to do that was to give civilization a wide berth. After three years however, and an increasing number of times where Adam was forced to brandish his technology in front of the locals, it would seem to suggest that the universe can handle us being here.

Afterall, if Tiamat can get away with stopping arrows with a wave of her hand, what could Adam and I possibly do that would hurt Earth's timeline?

> *He knows this planet's history better than I do. I'm sure he wouldn't be suggesting this without considering all the possibilities.*

"Ok, let's do it," I say tentatively, before adding with more conviction. "Let's make a better world!"

"That's my girl," he says, leaning in and kissing me passionately. He seems so confident all of a sudden. I think I could get used to this new Adam!

> *Maybe I should've run away earlier!*

I'm so lost in the moment that when his lips finally do pull away from mine, the three words I've been longing to say come spilling from my mouth unbidden.

"I love you," I tell him, breathlessly.

"I love you, too," he replies, grinning triumphantly.

Then dragging me up from the bed and into a loving, one-armed embrace, he adds: "And I'm gonna prove it, starting today!"

I'm the luckiest girl on this planet!

My face pressed against the warm grey leather of his jacket, I silently thank the Great Cosmic Scales for the blessings they have bestowed upon me. I'm free of the Paracas. My radiation poisoning is gone. And I have the man I love by my side. The future truly looks bright.

Maybe happily ever afters do exist after all...

To be continued...

ADAM NEXUS

Here is a sneak peek at a chapter from the third book in the Adam X universe, Adam Nexus. This is a prequel story to Adam Exiled, providing insight into some of the other characters left on the EDN after the escape of Adam Ten and Eve Eight. It begins 335 years before the creation of Adam Ten.

In this chapter we join Eldest, the Presever who presides over the EDN. You can pre-order Adam Nexus now. Simply head to the below link:

geni.us/AdamNexus

Chapter 1 – Book III
ELDEST

The moment is bittersweet. I watch silently as Adam Four continues to die slowly in the arms of Android Zero. He stares up at her unable to speak, while she waits for that last lingering spark of life in his eyes to fade to black.

Taking my own eyes from Adam and shifting them momentarily to the android, I watch her gently stroking his thinning grey hair with a care and compassion that I would never have thought possible. He loves her more than anything, of that I am certain. And if I didn't know better, I would swear she feels the same.

Truly she has surpassed her original programming in every way.

It has been quite the journey for all of us, I realise. For seventy human years, I have watched their story unfold, observing every moment of their life together. I know for a fact it never occurred to Adam Four that they were being watched.

He remained completely oblivious to my presence. I suspect Android Zero's highly attuned sensors may have alerted her that I was around once or twice.

Admittedly, seventy years is not particularly long when measured against the lifespan of a Preserver, but it is still the longest any of my kind has ever spent watching one specimen. A record I am certain will go uncelebrated by my peers.

My underlings think I'm obsessed.

They are probably correct. I will admit it is quite peculiar for an elder to spend so much time with a single specimen, let alone Eldest. But this was no ordinary case. There was no protocol in place to deal with a life form that continually took its own life, and I felt the problem was mine to solve. And so that is exactly what I did.

Android Zero has proved herself the perfect solution to my problem.

I pull my eyes from her and fix them back on Adam. His breathing has become laboured.

In the end, it had all been worth it. At least everything that happened after I left the inner ring and joined them in the Earth enclosure. The Enclosed Dimensional Nexus, while very useful for travelling through time and space, provided little in the way of privacy and I could hear the thoughts of other Preservers every time one of them passed too close to my observation pod. Their scrutiny and judgement was a constant distraction.

And the fact they knew I could hear them made their thoughts all the more frustrating.

I had to go. I simply had to place myself in the habitat itself so I could fully study homo sapien specimen four. That is why I requisitioned the Light Refraction Belt and took my leave.

The ancient piece of technology was wasting away in the Depository, an insufferable outcome for a device capable of rendering its wearer completely invisible. With it I had been able to enter Adam's enclosure and watch him up close. And in doing so, I freed myself from being constantly bombarded by the unwanted thoughts of my underlings.

> *They do not understand the pressure I face being in charge of such a gargantuan undertaking.*

In all of Preserver history, no Eldest has ever had a specimen take its own life and I had three do exactly that. All of them Adams. But where the first three clones were dismal failures, the fourth is an unparalleled success.

> *Or will be once he finally succumbs to death's inevitable embrace.*

Adam Four has lived a long and happy life, but all things must come to an end. There can be no greater outcome than dying of natural causes.

> *Finally, I will be able to resume leadership of the Enclosed Dimensional Nexus without being plagued by self-doubt.*

The admission comes unwelcomed, but I consider it all the same. I should be overjoyed that this one blemish on my otherwise spotless record is about to be corrected one and for all. But that argument crawls meekly to the back of my mind. Stuck in some recess and unable to escape.

Blocked.

Which is unusual given my ability to devote more than enough attention to multiple complex tasks at once.

Instead something else has me preoccupied and is pulling at my attention like a black hole might pull at a solar system. Looking down at Adam's old withered face, pride and achievement are kicked to the side by something deeper. Something primal and deemed more important by unexplored corners of my soul.

But I dare not identify these things, these feelings, welling up inside me now. Loss. Sadness. Grief. They're archaic, wasteful emotions. They will sow further self-doubt if I let them. But perhaps controlling them is now beyond my power. Even one as strong as I. They're an unstoppable force now, surging towards the surface. I have lost control of them.

Is it possible? Have I really come to care for this inferior creature?

The revelation stuns me, but as I watch him struggling to draw breath, I cannot deny that it is true. At some point during the last seven decades with Adam, I have clearly become attached to this remarkable specimen.

His waking sessions have provided me with countless hours of entertainment and, yes, introspection. There is no denying it.

Even asleep his unconscious mind was full of amusing content for me to unravel.

Thanks to the memory stamping process used on all clones, Adam Four had a perfect recollection of everything the original Adam Furst had experienced growing up on Earth. As a result, his head contains twenty-five years' worth of implanted information, all available to be sifted through while Android Zero and I would wait for him to wake up. And Earth, it seemed, was a complex place.

What joy I felt immersing myself in all aspects of its culture!

I found the most interesting of these memories to be his recollections of a subset of humans called actors. These fascinating individuals were like nothing I had ever witnessed before. A form of liar that appeared to be socially accepted by its peers, even though they pretended to be someone or something they were not.

They were even celebrated for their ability to perform this deception convincingly. The best among them being presented with shiny statuettes in recognition of their skills.

How odd that they would reward the best liars among them.

It was quite the conundrum. Lying was already a foreign concept for a Preserver, secrets being notoriously difficult to keep among a race of telepathic beings. But this newly discovered form of deception defied all logic.

These actors partook in a form of lying where the person being lied to was aware of the fact. Not only that, they even idolised the liar for deceiving them in such a way. It was a bizarre concept and at first glance it would seem totally pointless. But the Human mind seems to embrace itself in a way unique among the galaxies of this universe. To let one's imagination just be free for the sake of emotional cleansing is so brilliantly strange!

> *I suppose if unprobed, the strongest Preserver minds could theoretically keep information hidden from each other.*

Realistically, a simple omission is the best any of my people could hope to achieve, though. A Preserver relating anything other than the truth is completely unheard of, and one of our kind conveying a story that was anything less than factual even rarer.

> *If Preservers knew nothing of this new Human form of lying, what else is there that we do not know of? How can we preserve life if we don't yet fully understand what defines it?*

Sifting through Adam's memories, I became utterly enthralled with watching these actors play out their fictitious little stories. There was no shortage of options to enjoy. Movies. Television. Plays. These rank as some of the most exciting phenomena I have ever encountered inside a specimen's mind. I think I might miss these actors and actresses almost as much as I will miss the man himself.

Oh, how I would love to collect the one they call Meryl Streep for further analysis.

It is clear to me now that watching Adam Four overcome trials and tribulations for all these years has made me feel a certain kinship towards him. I may even consider him a friend.

Which is ridiculous when you consider he has no idea I even exist.

If I am being completely honest with myself, even Android Zero has come to hold a special place in my heart. I built her from scratch after the death of the first two Adams to serve as a caretaker and companion to all his future iterations. I am willing to admit I may have gotten a little carried away during the creation process.

Still, there is no arguing with the results!

Starting with the homo sapien genome as a template, I improved the skeletal design by using a crystal lattice composite instead of hardened calcium and invented synthetic skin that would give her increased healing and pliability. I then modelled her appearance on images taken from an odd series of publications Adam Furst kept under his bed during his adolescence.

*I still do not fully understand his fascination
with those pictures, or the ritual he would
engage in upon their viewing.*

But it was not until I created her plutonium powered
positronic brain that inspiration truly struck. Being
a human facsimile only used a fraction of that
magnificent mind, so I decided to add a few Preserver
traits to increase her overall intelligence and
functionality. By the time I was finished, she was able
to manipulate chronoton particles almost as well as
her creator.

*I never did get the quantum frequency issue
fully corrected, though.*

While she could open and travel through chronoton
portals herself – crossing large distances through
time, space and dimensions instantly – this flaw meant
anything organic she tried to transport would run the
risk of suffering an explosive cranial haemorrhage.
Although it was a non-issue really, since her job would
never require her to transport living creatures. Still, it
remained a flaw.

*The moving of specimens requires the gentle
touch of a Preserver. Not a machine designed
for protection and companionship.*

Despite this one inconsequential issue, the end result
was still a beautiful and sophisticated blend of Human
and Preserver. In fact, if I had chosen to give her the
ability to self-replicate, I may have had to classify her
as an entirely new life form rather than a lowly android.

However, like me she bounced back from her initial failure. The suicide of Adam Three spurred her to examine her own programming more closely and make adjustments accordingly. She shut off her ability to feel emotions and added a secondary function that had her remain silent rather than risk divulging information that could harm her specimen's psyche.

These new additions to her coding worked. She became the perfect companion to Adam Four, providing him the support he needed to survive these past seventy years.

Watching him now, laying there old and broken, labouring to draw breath through age-addled lungs, I find myself saddened by the sight. Everything must grow old and die. At least everything organic must.

My android could, potentially, last for ever.

Once again, I shift my gaze to her. Admiring the way she has allowed her hair to slowly lose pigment and her skin to wrinkle with time. It has provided the illusion that she has aged alongside Adam. This is, of course, all a charade. Another addition she made to her own programming for his benefit. She is truly ingenious.

*Admit it. This success is as much her doing
as it is mine.*

That thought comes unbidden and it's a revelation that threatens to consume my ongoing thoughts. But any attempt to analyse it is quickly derailed when Adam begins muttering something to her. With his waning strength, the words are little more than a whisper.

What is he saying?

Taking a big risk, I lean in close to the pair; closer than I have in seven decades. My curiosity is suddenly all consuming: I refuse to miss his final words. Not after everything we have been through together.

"My only regret is that I'm leaving you alone, love," Adam croaks, raising one gnarled hand to stroke Android Zero's wrinkled cheek. "Are you gonna be alright when I'm gone?"

The android nods her head. I notice she does so differently than usual. Slower, as if she knows she needs to look every bit the grieving partner as she cradles his head in her lap.

"Then I die a happy man," he finishes, burning the last of his energy and causing the last word to turn into a breathless sigh. There is one last tensing of his muscles, before his body goes limp and that final light in his eyes goes out.

It is done.

Android Zero reaches down and uses two fingers to close Adam's eyelids and I find an unexpected dampness building up around my own eyes. I was not aware my kind could cry, but it seems this specimen is still teaching me things I didn't know were possible.

> *This is the saddest thing I have ever seen.*
> *Even sadder than that animated film where*
> *the deer's mother was shot by a hunter.*

I recall Adam also found that movie particularly sad. I wipe the wetness from my eyes before it can spill over, then press a button on the LRB strapped around my waist. Shimmering for a moment the cloak deactivates, revealing me to Android Zero, who barely reacts to my sudden intrusion.

> *She knew I was here.*

Slowly she looks up from her charge, staring directly into my large obsidian eyes before speaking her first words in seventy years: "Did I perform my primary function to your satisfaction, Creator?"

Since our fifth law forbids me from communing directly with a lesser being, I mimic the nodding motion she used on Adam moments earlier. Acknowledging that this is as much praise as she is going to receive, she refrains from further questioning.

Lifting Adam's body, she carries it into the jungle to fulfil her last promise to him. A proper burial, as is customary among Humans, after which I am sure she will take time to reset her appearance in preparation for the fifth Adam's arrival.

> *I'm no longer needed here.*

The android has proven she can handle the clones. This has been a mostly pleasant diversion, but it really is time that I tend to other duties. After all, we still have an important mission to complete and an entire galaxy that needs preserving. I doubt the next Adam will be requiring my supervision.

My Second will surely be glad to have me resume command after such a long absence.

Still, as I use my mind to open a portal back to the inner ring of the EDN, I cannot help but wonder:

What other adventures might I miss now that I cannot spend all my free time watching the clones of Adam Furst?

I use my mind to open a portal back to the inner ring of the EDN, leaving Android Zero to bury the specimen. I'm ready to return to my duties.

My Second will surely be glad to have me resume command after such a long absence.

As soon as I step back into the inner ring, however, it's clear Second has been busy and it may not have been in my honour. A groundswell of negative thoughts hit me like a tidal wave, near knocking me to the ground.

Amongst the chaos that assaults my mind, one thought pushes its way through the din.

All is not well on the EDN.

Newsletter

We hope you enjoyed Adam Exiled and we're so thankful you took the time to read it. The good news is, this is only one book from a much larger series that, with your support, will span ten novels. That's right, Adam X is a far bigger universe than you imagine.

So if you have enjoyed Adam Exiled and would like us to go ahead and bring the whole series to life, all you need to do is **follow these simple steps**:

> *1.) Review and rate our book on stores like Amazon, Apple Books and Goodreads. The more reviews we see, the more we know you want to see more in the series.*

> *2.) Sign up to Nicholas Abdilla's newsletter to hear more about the next books, his favourite sci-fi moments, and many other goodies. This includes a bonus FREE copy of the excellent Game Guy comic. Sign up at **geni.us/adamX**.*

> *3.) Follow us on **Twitter**, on **Instagram** or on **Facebook** and share your thoughts and ideas about the Adam X universe. Just search for Old Mate Media.*

EXCYCLOPEDIA

Abe'L

[eyb-el]

person

The childhood cousin of Eve'E, Abe'L was a slave who worked the stem fields on Flora One. He died of radiation poisoning at a young age after being tricked into patching a core leak by his Paracas masters.

Adam Furst

[ad-uhm furst]

person

The homo sapien male chosen by the Preservers to represent his species on the EDN. Adam Furst lived on twenty-first century Earth and was a rookie police officer before his abduction. He now resides in a cryogenic stasis pod on board the Preservers' ship.

Adam 1

[ad-uhm wuhn]

person

The first clone of Adam Furst, he chose to kill himself by diving off a cliff rather than be held prisoner.

1. Also called **Adam I**

Adam 2

[ad-uhm too]

person

The second clone of Adam Furst, Adam II also chose
to kill himself by diving off a cliff rather than be held
prisoner be the Preservers.

1. Also called **Adam II**

Adam 3

[ad-uhm three]

person

The third clone of Adam Furst was given an android
protector, Android Zero. However, Android Zero was
too honest with Adam III regarding his location and
situation, so he eventually chose to asphyxiate himself
rather than be held prisoner by the Preservers.

1. Also called **Adam III**

Adam 4

[ad-uhm fawr]

person

The fourth clone of Adam Furst, Adam IV was the first
homo sapien clone considered to be a success by the
Preservers. He lived a long, happy life and died of old
age under the watchful gaze of his android protector
who, after failing with Adam III, had now taken a vow
of silence.

1. Also called **Adam IV**

Adam 5

[ad-uhm fahyv]

person

The fifth clone of Adam Furst, Adam V was mortally wounded and taken away from his android protector. Soon after the Preservers created a new homo sapien clone, leading the android to conclude Adam V must have perished.

1. Also called **Adam V**
2. Also called **homo sapien specimen 5**

Adam 6

[ad-uhm siks]

person

The sixth clone of Adam Furst, Adam VI lived a long and happy life that was brought to an end when he was bitten by a snake.

1. Also called **Adam VI**

Adam 7

[ad-uhm sev-uhn]

person

The seventh clone of Adam Furst, Adam VII lived a long and happy life that was brought to an end when he was mauled by a bear.

1. Also called **Adam VII**

Adam 8

[ad-uhm eyt]

person

The eighth clone of Adam Furst, Adam VIII lived a long and happy life that was brought to an end when he was eaten by a wolf.

1. Also called **Adam VIII**

Adam 9

[ad-uhm nahyn]

person

The ninth clone of Adam Furst, Adam IX lived a long and happy life that was brought to an end when he drowned in a river.

1. Also called **Adam IX**

Adam 10

[ad-uhm ten]

person

The tenth clone of Adam Furst, Adam X was the first clone to ever escape the Preservers. Unfortunately, when he landed back on Earth, he discovered the year was 4000BC, many millennia prior to the year in which his progenitor was abducted. He now struggles to build a new life for himself in what he considers the distant past.

1. Also called **Adam X**
2. Also called **homo sapien specimen 10**

Anne

[an]
person

An android created by the Preservers to help clones of Adam Furst adjust to life in captivity. After centuries of servitude, Anne turned on her creators and assisted Adam X in escaping his captors. Shortly after arriving on Earth, however, she faced a deadly threat and valiantly chose to sacrifice herself to save the man she had been programmed to protect and would later come to understand she loved.

Though missing for the last three years, it has recently become apparent that Anne may have survived the nuclear explosion in one form or another.

1. Also called **Android Zero**

Anthodaria

[an-thaw-dah-ree-ah]
fauna

A multi-coloured, underwater carnivore, Anthodaria spends its entire life rooted to one spot on the ocean floors of Oce'ana. They are able to catch food thanks to the use of their quick, tentacle-like tongue. Once the prey has been captured, it can be stored in the coral creature's stomach chamber for weeks, slowly being digested as needed.

Arganon

[ahr-gah-non]
place

The second planet orbiting a blue giant in the Orion system, Arganon has an equatorial diameter of 88729 miles (142796km), takes 452 days to complete a rotation around its sun, and has five moons. This forest world contains a wide assortment of flora and fauna, but nothing considered sentient.

Arganorse
[ahr-gah-nor-s]
fauna

Name given to a large, solid-hoofed, herbivorous quadruped by Adam X. Arganorse bears a strong resemblance to horses found on his Earth, with the only exception being it has green fur and four antlers that jut out at odd angles.

1. Also referred to as **Arganon quadruped 5521 specimen 5004**

Automaton
[aw-tom-uh-ton]
technology

Simple artificial servants created by the Preservers to perform menial tasks on board the EDN. Their use is mostly confined to the Core.

Battle 'Bot
[bat-l buht]
technology

Simple robot soldiers favoured by Paracas pirates as they search the galaxy for slaves. Battle 'Bots are

clunky and expensive, which is why most races still
prefer to use organic soldiers.

1. Also called **Paracas Battle 'Bot**

Brien
[brahy-uhn]
person

The first homo sapien enslaved by the Paracas, Brien
lived on Earth in the fortieth century BC. A pig farmer
on a remote Scottish isle, Brien is a short man with
red hair and a thick red beard. He is also mute, as his
tongue was cut out as a youth. Brien is also an ancient
ancestor to Eve'E.

Buudaki
[boo-duh-ki]
place

The first planet orbiting a red giant in the Flora system,
Buudaki has an equatorial diameter of 32600 miles
(56460km), takes 219 days to complete a rotation
around its sun, has an asteroid ring, and one moon.
This desert world also contains a small assortment of
subterranean fauna found just beneath its surface.

Captain Albright
[kap-tuhn awl-brahyt]
person

The grizzled, old police captain in charge of officers
Adam Furst and Frank Morningstar on Earth. Captain
Albright is not a fan of Adam Furst, sending him on

forced leave the day he was abducted for reasons that remain unclear.

Chronoton
[kron-oh-ton]
physics

Chronotons are exotic particles that were created during the Big Bang and when properly manipulated can allow one to see, hear or even move through time. This subatomic particle exists almost everywhere and is invisible to electromagnetic radiation.

Chronoton Burn
[kron-oh-ton burn]
physics

A reaction of heat and light that can be observed when an inanimate object is being erased from existence. Chronoton burn is caused by the movement of agitated chronoton particles and occurs when history is being rewritten.

1. Also called Chrono-burn

Cloud Stinger
[kloud sting-er]
fauna

A small, gelatinous invertebrate. Cloud Stingers are capable of flight thanks to their helium-filled hoods. They have umbrella-like bodies and tentacles they use to feed on prey. While originally from Arganon, Cloud Stingers have spread to numerous worlds thanks to their ability to survive in the vacuum of space riding on the cosmic winds, and a tendency to attach themselves to starship hulls.

Core

[kawr]
place

The very centre of the Preservers ship, the EDN, the Core consists of multiple levels containing cryogenics, propulsion, life support and the depository. The large spherical structure is run by automatons, meaning Preservers are free to focus on other tasks.

Cryogenics

[krahy-uh-jen-iks]
place

A section inside the Core of the Preservers' Enclosed Dimensional Nexus ship where all abductees are cryogenically frozen after having their DNA harvested for cloning.

Danu

[dah-noo]
person

An ancient Celtic goddess, Danu is said to be the mother of all the gods. She is also the goddess said to represent earth, fertility, wisdom and wind.

1. Also called **Danu the Divine**

Depository

[dih-poz-i-tawr-ee]
place

A section inside the Preserver ship's Core where all abductees' personal possessions are stored.

Drop Pod

[drop pod]
vehicle

A small, one being escape pod located in the outer ring of the EDN. Drop pods are transparent spheres that are programmed to disintegrate upon landing to prevent Preserver technology from being studied by other beings.

1. Also called **escape pod**

Eldest

[el-dist]
person

Name given to the oldest Preserver on board the EDN. A member of the ruling Trinity.

1. Also called **Elder**

Elixir

[ih-lik-ser]
chemical

An illegal narcotic created and sold by the Paracas race, using pollen processed be slaves on Flora One.

It is known to put those who use it into an incredible state of euphoria.

Elvee
[el-vee]
place

The sixth planet orbiting a yellow star in the Oce system, Elvee has an equatorial diameter of 864000 miles (1.4 million km), takes a whopping 1213 days to complete a rotation around its sun, and has twenty-one moons. This gaseous world has a wide assortment of specialised fauna designed to survive in its methane atmosphere.

Enclosed Dimensional Nexus
[en-klohzd dih-men-shuhnl nek-suhs]
vehicle

This Preserver vessel is the most sophisticated spacecraft ever created. The inner and outer rings that comprise a large portion of the Enclosed Dimensional Nexus rotate perpendicular to one another at such high velocity that the vessel resembles a large sphere of light when viewed from the outside.

While the ship has an equatorial diameter of 87 miles (140km) in real space, it actually has infinite room within thanks to its ability to create and hold pocket dimensions within its spinning rings.

1. Also called **EDN**

Eve 8

[eev eyt]

person

The eighth clone of the original Eve'E Floran abducted
by the Preservers, Adam X rescued her while making
his own escape. Eve'E was traumatised by her time
on board the Preserver ship, refusing to speak a word
until they had landed safely on Earth. Better known as
Eve, her name has also been mistaken as Evie.

1. Also called **Spock**
2. Also called **homo florus specimen 8**
3. Also called **Eve'E**
4. Also called **Evie**

Exile

[eg-zahyl]

person

Name given to a Preserver Eldest after being exiled
from the EDN.

Fire lizard

[fahyuhr liz-erd]

fauna

Refers to any of the large reptiles capable of flight and
breathing fire that are found on varying planets across
the galaxy. Fire lizards come in a variety of colours
depending on their world of origin, with some – like
the green species found on Flora One – having been
mercilessly hunted into extinction. Despite being the
apex predator of that world, the fearsome creatures

were no match for the superior technology and weapons used by the invading Paracas. Fire lizards also bear a striking resemblance to the mythological dragons of Earth.

1. Also called **Floran fire-lizard**

Flora One
[flawr-uh wuhn]
place

The first planet orbiting a yellow star in the Flora system, Flora One has an equatorial diameter of 7521 miles (12104km), takes 370 days to complete a rotation around its sun, and has two moons. This garden world contains a wide assortment of giant flora and is prevalent in the production of many illicit drugs sold throughout the galaxy.

Floran
[flawr-in]
people

A slave race with shared origins to modern-day home sapiens. However, they were abducted from Earth by the Paracas and relocated to the planet of Flora One. Florans still resemble their human ancestors except for one notable exception. Years of selective breeding and genetic tampering to improve their resilience to their new environment has caused Floran ears to develop a slight point at their tops.

1. Also called **homo florus**

Frank Morningstar

[frangk mawr-ning-stahr]
person

The senior police officer who was partnered with
rookie officer Adam Furst shortly after his graduation
on Earth. Frank Morningstar is a balding, middle-aged
man with a thick black moustache and a fun-loving
sense of humour.

Great Cosmic Scales

[greyt koz-mik skeylz]
religion

A popular religion practiced on many worlds across
the Milky Way galaxy. The Great Cosmic Scales
originated with the monks of Buudaki, who spoke of a
universal balance represented by a set of scales. They
preached these Great Cosmic Scales would tip back
and forth between good and bad, meaning you could
never remain in one state or the other forever. Those
who believe in the Great Cosmic Scales find hope in
the faith that nothing can be good or bad for ever.

Hela

[hel-uh]
1. *place*

The only planet orbiting a binary star in the Hades
system, Hela has a diameter of just 2160 miles
(3476km) and takes 686 days to complete a rotation
around its suns. This world is covered by an ocean of
lava and plays host to the Olympian Alliance's most
notorious prison.

2. *vulgarity*

A curse word used to express something unpleasant.

Henrietta Furst
[hen-ree-et-uh furst]
person

The mother of Adam Furst. Henrietta Furst married Nigel Mann after Adam's father passed away. She has greying, blonde hair and was last known to be living in Munich, Germany.

Hunger
[huhng-ger]
fauna

A deadly macroscopic virus of unknown origin. This gelatinous metamorphic entity will only attack creatures smaller than itself, but increases in mass every time it does so. There is no limit to how large it can grow, but it does have an aversion to fire and can be burned back down to size.

While communicating with The Hunger appears to be impossible, it does show signs of intelligence. It has displayed an ability to recognise danger and restrain its own ravenous appetite if food sources become scarce.

1. Also called **White Death**
2. Also called The Hunger

Inner Ring

[in-er ring]
place

A spinning ring with an equatorial diameter of 86 miles (138km), this is the nerve centre of the Preservers' ship, the EDN. This portion of the craft is where the Preservers observe their artificial habitats and clone specimens. Preservers rarely leave the inner ring.

Kaa'lik

[key-lik]
1. *place*

The first planet orbiting a white dwarf in the Krés cluster, Kaa'lik has an equatorial diameter of 2100 miles (3300km) and takes 150 days to complete a rotation around its sun. This volcanic world is home to a hive of spacefaring insects of the same name.

2. *fauna*

A swarm of large spacefaring insects, a Kaa'lik hive is made up primarily of male drones who can be telepathically controlled over great distances by a queen. As a Kaa'lik's diet consists mostly of metal, they have been known to attack starships en masse. They have also been known to capture organic crew members for their queen so she can use their bodies as incubators for her eggs. Kaa'lik bear a striking resemblance to the praying mantis of Earth, and while the average drone stands at around six-feet-tall, a queen can grow to twice that size.

Kai'N

[key-en]

person

The father of Eve'E, Kai'N was a slave who worked the stem fields on Flora One. He was also a strong believer in the Great Cosmic Scales, a deeply held faith he shared with his daughter.

Khufu

[koo-foo]

person

An Egyptian man who lived on Earth in the fortieth century BC, Khufu was a tribal warrior who hunts predominantly in areas surrounding the Nile River. He is also the oldest friend of the tribe's leader, Sobek, and his most loyal soldier.

Kréken

[krey-ken]

people

A race of amphibious warriors. Kréken live to hunt and will often wear pieces of those they have slain. They're also fiercely loyal to those they deem worthy. Kréken can grow up to eight-feet-tall, have light blue skin, four eyes and tentacles which protrude from the back of their heads.

1. Also called **Krékarus**

Krés

[krey-s]
place

The fifth planet orbiting a white dwarf in the Krés cluster, Krés has an equatorial diameter of 74600 miles (120000km), takes 675 days to complete a rotation around its sun, and has three moons.

This frozen world contains a subterranean ocean as an icy crust that covers the entire surface. There's consistent snowfall all year round.

Lonsdaleite

[lonz-deyl-ahyt]
mineral

A hexagonal-dihexagonal dipyramidal mineral containing carbon. Lonsdaleite is approximately fifty times stronger than diamond and has a melting point well above 3632°F (2000°C). It is also the mineral primarily used to construct the latest Preserver technology, including automatons. It was also used when growing Android Zero's skeletal structure.

Median

[med-ee-uhn]
people

An aquatic race of healers known to have created nanites and the universal translator. Not too much is known about their history.

Memory Stamping
[mem-uh-ree stamp-ing]
technology

A device which makes an exact copy of a host's memories and transfers them into a clone. This process is used for both newly cloned Preservers and newly cloned specimens. With the latter the clone is rarely aware that their memories aren't their own. The first specimen to discover they had been the subject of memory stamping was a home sapien.

Meryneith
[mer-ee-neeth]
person

An Egyptian man who lived on Earth in the fortieth century BC, Meryneith was a tribal warrior who hunted predominantly in areas surrounding the Nile River. He was also the son of the tribe's leader, Sobek, and was a close friend of Khufu.

1. Also called **Mery**

Mushroots
[muhsh-roots]
flora

Small, edible fungi commonly found on Flora One. Mushroots have a thin, yet sturdy stem and a bulbous head covered in spots. They require darkness and moisture to grow and are usually found at the base of queenspire flower stems.

Nanites

[nan-ahytz]
technology

These are microscopic, self-replicating robots created by the Medians. Once introduced to a patient's bloodstream, nanites can heal most wounds and even purge a body of corruptions, including radiation.

Nigel Mann

[nahy-juhl man]
person

A Brigadier in the British Armed Forces, Nigel Mann married single mother Henrietta Furst. He helped raise Adam Furst during his formative years, but in the end, divorced his mother for reasons unknown.

Nyx

[niks]
group

A highly respected clan found on Krés, they are led by a matriarch called Nyx. The Kréken warrior Zanatos is known to be a member of this group.

Oce'ana

[oh-shee-an-uh]
place

The fourth moon orbiting a gas giant in the Oce system, Oce'ana has an equatorial diameter of 37300 miles (60000km) and a 38-hour orbit. The ocean moon is teeming with aquatic flora and fauna.

Olympian Alliance

[uh-lim-pee-uhn uh-lahy-uhns]

group

An organisation made up of 12 allied species, the Olympian Alliance enforces law and order in the Milky Way galaxy.

Outer Ring

[ou-ter ring]

place

A spinning ring with an equatorial diameter of 87 miles (140km), this section represents the very edge of the Preservers' ship, the EDN. This portion of the craft is where the Drop Pods are housed and is rarely visited by Preservers.

Overlord

[oh-ver-lawrd]

person

The leader of a criminal organisation that engages in the trafficking of illegal narcotics and slave labour throughout the Milky Way galaxy.

Paracas

[pah-rak-es]

people

A race of greedy opportunists, the Paracas are known to have few scruples when it comes to turning a profit. They have a stranglehold on the galactic black market, selling everything from weapons to narcotics and even people. Paracas can grow up to eight-feet-tall, partially due to their abnormally long craniums. They have bright orange skin, and their eyes can range in colour from vibrant yellow to blood red.

Peacekeeper
[pees-kee-per]
technology

A type of plasma pistol used by those serving in the Olympian Alliance. Two Peacekeepers were stolen from the EDN's depository and given to Adam X. This weapon also has the ability to both kill and stun depending on which power pack is loaded.

Preservers
[pri-zurv-ers]
people

A race of telepathic and telekinetic time travellers. Preservers have made it their mission to preserve one of every lifeform in the galaxy for a reason known only to them. They reproduce via cloning and as such, each one is exactly four-feet-tall, grey skinned, and has a bulbous head with large obsidian eyes.

Pulse Emitter
[puhls ih-mit-er]
technology

A device inside of Anne's positronic brain which allows her to open portals through time, space and dimension. Her pulse emitter requires 10 Earth hours of charging after every use.

Queenspire

[kween-spahyuhr]

flora

An enormous wildflower commonly found on Flora One. The queenspire has bright, yellow petals and a large, green stem that can grow up to 100 feet tall. Its pollen can also be used to create the illegal, mind-altering drug known as Elixir.

Rigilius Asteroid

[rahy-jil-ee-es as-tuh-roid]

place

Any of the thousands of rocks ranging from 480 miles (775 km) to less than one mile (1.6km) in diameter that orbit the Rigiluis star. This belt is home to a wide range of tiny, spacefaring insects and is a common feeding ground to one species of slow-moving tardigrade.

Sap-Sucker

[sap suhk-er]

fauna

A long, multilegged insect that feeds on the sticky ooze found inside flower stems. Sap-suckers are commonplace in the stem fields of Flora One.

Second

[sek-uhnd]

person

Name given to the second oldest Preserver on board the EDN. A member of the ruling Trinity.

Shock Collar
[shok kol-er]
technology

A device used by the Paracas to punish their workforce, these collars were locked around the necks of every slave and could be used to shock those who displeased their masters.

Skitter-Bug
[skit-er buhg]
fauna

A small, six-legged insect that feeds on faecal matter and other organic waste, Skitter-bugs are nocturnal creatures hiding underground during the day and feeding at night.

Sobek
[soh-bek]
person

An Egyptian man who lived on Earth in the fortieth century BC, Sobek was the leader of a warrior tribe who hunted predominantly in areas surrounding the Nile River. He also had a son named Meryneith.

Stem-Hopper
[stem hop-er]
fauna

A small, carnivorous mammal with large floppy ears, stem-hoppers are capable of jumping great distances. Native to Flora One, they also have a large tusk protruding from their bottom jaw, which they use to impale their prey.

Synthetic Flesh
[sin-thet-ik flesh]
technology

The flesh-like substitute used to cover Android Zero's skeletal frame giving her the appearance of a homo sapien. Synthetic flesh regenerates much like regular flesh through the consumption of organic matter. Its superior design, however, means it does so at a much faster rate than Human skin.

1. Also called **synth-flesh**

Tiamat
[tyah-maht]
person

An ancient Babylonian goddess, Tiamat is said to be the mother of all the gods. She is also the goddess said to represent the sea.

1. Also called **Tiamat the Water Serpent**
2. Also called **Tee**

Third
[thurd]
person

Name given to the third oldest Preserver on board the EDN. A member of the ruling Trinity.

Trident
[trahyd-nt]
vehicle

A type of spacecraft flown by those serving in the
Olympian Alliance.

Trinity
[trin-i-tee]
group

A group that consists of the three oldest Preservers.
These individuals are responsible for all decisions
made on board the EDN.

Universal Translator
[yoo-nuh-vur-suhl trans-ley-ter]
technology

A small device able to translate any language
spoken into it into the one required by the wearer.
The technology was created by the Medians. Anne
attached the universal translator to a glove so it could
be worn by Adam X during their escape from the
Enclosed Dimensional Nexus.

The Universal Translator Glove was last seen in
possession of Adam X on the surface of Earth in the
fortieth century BC.

1. Also called **UT**
2. Also called **UTG**

Youngest

[yuhng-gist]
person

Name given to the most recently cloned Preserver on
board the EDN.

1. Also called **Young One**

Zanatos

[zan-ah-toh-s]
person

A clone of the original Kréken abducted by the
Preservers, Zanatos attacked Adam X and Anne, but
was defeated by them. After Adam chose to spare his
life, clan custom demanded he serve the man until he
could regain his honour. Unfortunately, Zanatos got left
behind during Adam's chaotic escape from the EDN,
but a recording sent to him afterwards seemed to
suggest he found his own way to securing freedom.

1. Also called **Zee**

ABOUT THE CREATOR

Who is Nicholas Abdilla?

Hello and thank you for immersing yourself in my Adam X universe. I hope you're enjoying it! However, you should know it's far from my first creative work. I've been writing and drawing comics since the age of four! Although, as you can imagine, my early stuff was not so great.

My dad was an artist you see, so he was a major influence and inspiration for me in first putting pencil to paper. But the thing is, I also loved to tell stories.

Through these two passions, I gradually became obsessed with comic books as a storytelling medium. I never took any specific classes as I grew up, instead just developing my skills through practice. Hours and hours; day after day.

Both my primary and secondary schools where always very encouraging when it came to writing and drawing. I won various awards for my efforts, which was great. But my proudest moments were when my works were put into our school libraries.

The positive feedback from my peers was instrumental in giving me the confidence I needed to put myself out there and to never give up.

At age 15, I decided I needed a brand name for my collection of books, and Nick Ab's Comix was born. When school was over, I registered the name Nick Ab's Comix and took my work online. I spent a long time trying to build up a fan base on MySpace, and later (and still) on Facebook.

I posted content to the site weekly, and the adventures of Adam X became my largest ongoing series. Once I'd clocked up some decent numbers, I felt brave enough to try approaching other companies to see if they liked my work.

I was over the moon when I got picked up by my favourite magazine, *Game Informer*. It was the fastest growing magazine in Australia at the time. I worked on a comic strip called *Game Guy* for them, which appeared every month for the next few years.

However, when that ended, I realised I'd neglected some of my other stories.

I decided I wanted to move away from comics for a while and write my first true novel. Choosing Adam X as the star of that book was an easy decision, as I had invested so much in the lore and the story.

I had a full ten book narrative arc already mapped out, so there was a considerable body of work focused around Adam already in existence. It felt only natural to turn that into my first series of novels.

And here we are! Book two, *Adam Exitus*, is out and available across the world! It joins *Adam Exiled*, and a third entry, *Adam Nexus*, will also land in 2020.

Thank you again for taking the time to read my series. I hope you've enjoyed it, and would love to hear your thoughts in the reviews on your store of purchase, and/or through social.

This will be influential in how things pan out with future books in the series, which I am busy working on right now. So until then, stay safe and be happy!

*If you'd like to learn more about Nicholas Abdilla, you can **read an interview** over at the www.oldmatemedia.com website.*

*You can also follow Nicholas Abdilla directly at; **facebook.com/nickabscomix/***

Make sure you get all the books in the ever-expanding
Adam X universe.

BOOK I
Adam Exitus

BOOK 3
Adam Nexus

GO TO
geni.us/AdamX

WHERE TO NEXT?

Looking for another great read? Why not try another title from the **Old Mate Media** catalogue; visit...

www.oldmatemedia.com/shop

REALISE YOUR
WRITING DREAMS

Did you know we work with indie authors and individuals who dream of publishing their own stories? Find out more about how we can bring your words to life and read our huge range of free publishing guides at **oldmatemedia.com** or via one of our social channels.

 /OLDMATEMEDIA

 @OLDMATEMEDIA

 /OLDMATEMEDIA

9 781925 638691